The Many Beautiful Worlds

of

Death

The Many Beautiful Worlds

of

Death

A fantastical tale of adventure

by

Mark Sheeky

Pentangel Books

The Many Beautiful Worlds of Death written by Mark Sheeky.
Illustrations and graphic design by Mark Sheeky.

2nd edition, published in 2021 by Pentangel Books.
www.pentangel.co.uk
ISBN 978-1-9999800-3-0

Copyright ©2021 by Mark Sheeky.

Mark Sheeky asserts his right to be identified as the author of this work in
accordance to the Copyright, Designs and Patents act of 1988.

Chapter One

Ripped gold hair
forms a ring in the sky,
burning the air
like a saw-blade eye.

Dark heavy disc, hangs.
Leather green tongues of leaf.
I kneel at your limp yellow hands,
and pray beneath.

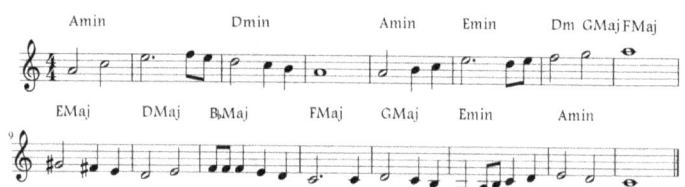

Chapter Two

"About six weeks," said the doctor. "It's hard to say. We don't like to say. Everyone is different. But not long. Not six months. Although that happens sometimes. Rarely. Six weeks is typical."

The office was decorated in pale neutral hues, and the effervescent glow from the porthole window to the right lit up a desert plant, gently nodding like a ballerina taking a bow. George was distracting himself. He had expected bad news. The pain in his head was quite specific in location, and his brief research into brain tumours was not positive. George knew he was probably going to die but he didn't want to accept it. He didn't want to be told because that would make it true. He didn't want his heart to feel that it was true. He didn't want to feel and know that he was going to die, soon.

"I'm sorry," said Doctor Price with sympathy. "We can offer counselling; in fact I recommend it. Talking about these things often helps and it's important to accept it so that you can plan for the future."

"Are you sure that nothing can be done?" asked George meekly. He looked into the eyes of the doctor as he spoke, to be sure, to absorb each fragment of communication.

"We can't help. I'm very sorry, you are going to die."

For a microsecond Doctor Price's cool professional resolve cracked and a shot of sadness sliced at George. He felt it and looked away. There's something so final about the word "die". "We're all dying." That's what his mum used to say when George complained. She was right. But George was dying more quickly than most.

A stabbing pain exploded on the left side of his head, making him wince and gulp, like a boy with a mouthful of horrid medicinal brandy.

"I'll give you something for the pain," said the doctor. He turned to his terminal and tapped out a prescription. "You'll probably need something stronger later. I'll give you something to help you sleep too." Tap tap tap. Print. Rip. "Here."

The distant plant was conducting a waltz now, a gentle waft in time to the pulses of air from the air conditioner below. George was thinking about the forgotten friends at his school leaver's disco, and the summer. It was the first truly beautiful day of the year today and for all George knew it would be the last beautiful day he would see. No more Christmases. Actually, no more birthdays either. He would die aged twenty-nine.

The doctor was talking about appointments at clinics or hospitals or something. "Thank you for telling me straight, doctor," said George, standing up. "I'll go now. Thank you."

He shook the doctor's hand and took the prescription, then turned and left. Everything seemed different than before. Time seemed liquid, pulsing like the plant. Colours seemed more vivid, and the air tasted more fresh. The moment would have been perfect if it wasn't for the throbbing in the side of his head. And the impending death. George badly wanted a cup of tea.

He sauntered through the waiting room, ignoring the reception desk. Any appointments can wait until he had decided what to do. George didn't like doctors. Doctors seemed to consider themselves slightly higher in the evolutionary chain than ordinary people. Their special piece of paper, so hard earned in the years of medical college, was like a magic ticket that proved their superiority. Doctors knew best. Other doctors, however, knew with certainty that they were better than their colleagues, and consultants considered all general practitioners buffoons, as well as their colleagues.

The glass doors slid majestically and silently open to reveal every joy of summer. The surgery was fronted by the most beautiful garden. A short lawn of a few metres circled the clean, modern building like a soft moat, its certain warmness inviting the bare feet it would probably never experience.

George saw a red and black butterfly on a pink rose outside. It was lying there sunning itself. He paused and watched it flex its wings for a few seconds.

"I will live longer than you," he thought, attempting self-comfort. He flashed a smile, took a sharp breath in, and began to walk home in the sun. The butterfly took flight and spiralled around a mate, the two playing like children without worry or care.

At home, Pauline was tending her sunflowers in the garden. She was kneeling on a pad and inspecting the leaves for problems, lifting each one delicately with her pink rubber-gloved hands. After a loving gaze, each leaf was wiped with a damp cloth to clean it and carefully let go.

"Beautiful day, isn't it?" came a call. It was Roger Castavet, the handsome next door neighbour. He was standing in the shade near the fence holding some hand shears, sleeves rolled up in preparation for some work. Roger was about George's age and looked like him too. Roger's wife had muscular dystrophy and she rarely came out. Sometimes her bony shadow, like a lonely shark, would float in the dark depths beyond the French windows, her electric wheelchair on patrol. Roger tried not to talk about her much, although a lot of his life revolved around her care. Her diagnosis changed Roger's life as much as hers, but he seemed as content and loving as he would have been bringing up a family, as they had once planned to do.

"Isn't it marvellous!?" cried Pauline, standing up for a break. "The first proper day of summer. My babies are loving it!" She looked up at the tallest flower, its head eclipsing the sun in a gentle affirmative nod.

"It is," said Roger with a sideways smile. "The perfect day to not do any gardening! I've got to do this lawn though." There was a slight pause. "How is George doing?"

George's headaches and subsequent tests were not a secret.

"He's due back any moment," replied the ever optimistic Pauline with an upward head movement. Roger made a comforting smile: "You'll be alright."

Near her feet, a fat bee meandered and swerved through beams of grass like a World War Two bomber dodging towers of flak, its crystalline eye fixed upon the alluring golden target of a distant buttercup. It circled the flower a few times, identifying the ideal spot, then gripped onto its lolling head, which was far too tiny for its bulbous body, causing the flower to droop alarmingly, before the bee released its grip, and tumbled unmajestically earthwards.

The peace was disturbed by a metallic clatter from the conservatory. The domed building of glass and white P.V.C. made a web-like structure that jutted out into the lawn, gripping at its heart like a giant skeletal hand. Inside, amongst a spatter of white plastic furniture and a cascade of music discs, was Adam, the mechanical child of George and Pauline. George was sterile, and after years of trying to have a natural child they had decided to construct one.

Adam was squatting amidst the pile of discs, trying to pick up the smooth boxes with his clumsy wooden hands. The circular-saw blade in his chest spun rapidly in panicked agitation, making an intermittent grating sound. When he got really excited it made sparks that flew out of the pizza-slice hole where his sternum would be if he were a real boy.

His head darted left and right, mirroring the robotic movements of his arms. Grasping, stacking, sliding, and using his legs as barriers to help lift the flimsy boxes with his hard pine digits.

"Adam - what have you done!?" cried Pauline with a smile from the lawn.

"It - they just fell over," said Adam in his flat, grey voice. His actions became more frantic when his mother spoke. His arm suddenly shot out, causing a transparent case to shoot across the amber stone tiles with a clattering hiss like a jazz drummer's exhale.

Pauline was only feigning annoyance at this trivial accident, and she stepped into the conservatory, peeling off her gloves and bending down to help pick up the discs. "Come on, let's put them all back."

Adam had difficulty understanding irony or sarcasm because he didn't have emotions. Adam's brain wasn't sophisticated enough to fully comprehend humans, and this was often a source of frustration to him and to those around him. He had lots of friends, but he would never truly understand them. Each of his actions was the result of a list of rules, each rule etched into his copper brain by an experience. Rules of ever increasing complexity that struggled to cope with each situation, like a book of every possible chess board, while the meaning of the game remained ever elusive, and the joy of playing ever unknowable.

Mother and son soon stacked the discs and placed them neatly on a small light bamboo table that sat lovingly next to the silver plastic player.

The distinctive sound of the front gate heralded the arrival of

George. The sweeping front lawn was bisected by a light stone path that led from the white metal gate to the dark-green front door. The back garden was actually on the right side of the detached house, behind a tall hedge, with a wooden gate that occupied an arched hole in the centre. Fantastic webs filled with huge garden spiders populated the top of the arch in late summer, making it advisable to duck when moving from the front lawn to the back.

The gate opened and Adam came running out with a jolting gait. "Daddy! I've been trying to play music but I kept dropping everything! I've been so bored today. Will I have a new brother soon?"

He was talking about David. George thought about the second child. Half of his parts were strewn about the desk of his workshop amidst the plans. He hadn't thought of it before but he won't have time to complete him now. Adam would probably remain alone.

"Perhaps one day..." said George wistfully. He sighed and blinked slowly. He suddenly felt very sad.

He had expected to be told that he would die. Even when the doctors told him that there was a decent chance that the tumour would be operable, he had expected it wasn't. It felt bad. He wasn't prepared to tell the people he loved, though. Suddenly it felt worse to tell them than to know it himself.

"Perhaps one day you'll learn how to make a brother for yourself." He tapped Adam on his hard shoulder. "Where is your mother? I have to talk to her. I have to talk to both of you."

The pair ducked through the dark arch into the new summer of the back garden. Pauline had her back to the gate, and was now leaning on the distant fence, talking intimately with Roger, who was a safe bed of flowers away on his side. She giggled through her nose at some unheard joke, and turned, still overtly happy, to see George and Adam appear. George looked awful. Roger raised an uncomfortable nod of acknowledgement before turning away to return to his task, bending down and clipping the rim of his lawn with tiny shears, trying to make the edge all perfect but never quite being satisfied.

George was anxious to break the news. He went into the conservatory with Adam, and Pauline followed, carrying the neat yellow tools that she reserved for her sacred acts of sunflower care. She put the things down and stood to face George.

"They can't do anything. I have about six weeks. Well, probably." His words were filled with sadness. "They can't do anything, anyway." He blinked damp eyes and the pair embraced. "I'm sorry." A gulp of emotion filled his chest and flowed upwards. They paused for a long second. The only sound was the gentle rhythmic purr of Adam's heart.

George sighed and pulled back, wiping his eyelids with his fingers. Pauline swallowed.

Adam was standing, watching. "Why are you sad?" he enquired in his ever soothing monotone. He recognised that tears meant sadness.

"I'm going to die soon. I'm sad because I will have to leave you and your mother," responded George using language that Adam would understand best.

"But, I thought everybody died? Like Pansy."

Pansy was Adam's hamster. Pansy lived in a small cage, with a green plastic bottom sprinkled with wood shavings, in a corner of Adam's bedroom. He nibbled flakes of hamster food, sipped droplets of water from the steel ball of the dispenser, and he ran around his wheel; round and round and round and going nowhere. Then he died. He never saw another hamster, or did anything beyond his universal experience of food and water and wheel. So it goes.

"It's better to know when you will die than not," said Adam, confused. "I'd rather know when, than not."

Adam thought that George's tears were for George.

"You are a very special person," said George, giving up the argument. Adam would never know or understand death. It was something that only living creatures know about, an inherent fear, a spectral companion. Adam might live forever. Ironic, that the only creature that was perfectly at peace with the thought of his own death was as good as immortal. Adam clattered away towards the kitchen and living room beyond.

The talk with Adam had calmed George down and pulled him back from the warm, soft rooms of emotion to the angular minimalism of the intellect.

"We must ask the flowers for help!" enthused Pauline, her widened eyes moved to the sunflower's face and she meandered out, like the bee. George stepped into the house, thorough the gap that was home to the heavy door that separated kitchen from conservatory. He filled the domed chromium kettle with water from the tap and clicked the switch. The kettle growled as it began to wrestle the cold water into hot.

Pauline talked to the sunflowers daily. George used to work so hard and was away all of the time, especially when they were first married and short of money. Pauline needed more friends, and the sunflowers became something of a substitute. Her mother Ursula used to have a vast country garden, and as a small girl Pauline would love to help her, tending to her own special flowers as though they were her children. She always had a magic touch with plants, almost to sense what they were thinking, what they needed. She often told George that they talk to her more than she talks to them, and he believed her. Her sunflowers were special friends; she had always had at least one. The first was a present when she was very small, but each year she grew a new one, and when they died gave them a proper funeral.

George sipped his delicious tea. A plop of pain belched behind his eye socket making him grimace.

Pauline burst in like a dove into sun. "They said that you will survive!" she beamed. "They are never wrong! Those doctors don't know what they were talking about. They've missed something. I knew they would! Oh I'm so happy!"

She kissed George's face making him shudder into wakefulness and began to hum tum tum and bounce around the kitchen like a ping-pong ball in love. She juggled her favourite fine china cup off the wall and tossed a teabag in followed by a shiny spoon that tinkled home like an angel's "Hallelujah!"

George took a sip and made a fist. "You're right. I don't want to die. I am a genius. I can solve any problem! Nobody on Earth has my skill and ability!"

"Yes! Yes!" sang Pauline, "You can cure yourself."

"Maybe..." he mused, more pragmatically. "Maybe not me, but maybe somebody can. My portal is nearly complete. I can use it to find someone with the answer. I've got six weeks. Six long..."

A sudden stab of pain cut him short. He winced and contorted his face, scrunching his eyes into a tight ball and raking eight claw-like fingers tightly down his forehead to his vice-like jaw. The pain eased.

"I've nothing to lose." he said quietly, and sipped a welcome mouthful of tea.

Pauline rushed over and put her arm around his shoulders.

"Everything's going to be all right. You'll see," she said quietly. "I'm alright." He blinked and kissed his wife gently on the cheek.

Pauline stood up and took a breath. Her focus instantly shifted to making her tea and her regular browse through the pages of the Mottley James gardening catalogue. She plonked down at the kitchen table and flicked though the book with a laser focus, licking the occasional index finger and humming to herself, pausing only to sip her particularly favoured Assam blend.

In the basement, the strip-lights flickered into life with a joyous tone, humming their yellow-green optimism above the rich wood that decked the periphery of the workshop. The walls of the room looked like the lower deck of a Spanish galleon, yet with a tangle of thick electrical cables that spewed from occasional recesses like living liquorice. This was George's experiment room, the portal room, a place that was once piled high with household junk and the inevitable detritus of nearly a decade of modern living, but that three years or so ago had been converted into a laboratory.

"On!" he spoke, in a tone like Ali-Baba commanding an unseen deity. There was a whirring sound, and more lights blinked into existence. The distant third of the room suddenly became animated, as polished black obelisks with crisp glass outlines awoke in a spatter of tiny red lights.

"Primary systems initiated," said a cold female voice. The hard-disc drives inside the supercomputer ticked like nervous beetles. The atmospheric conditioning units began to warm and dry and purify, their robot throats heaving in dust and dampness, and heaving out a dry mix of seventy-eight point zero nine percent nitrogen, twenty point nine five percent oxygen, and the other gasses of an ideal air.

George hadn't been here in three weeks, not since his illness began, and the tests, and the worry. Perhaps this machine had caused it. Who can say? He blew away a fine layer of dust from the hand rail and stepped down the creaking wooden stairs.

In the middle of the room was a huge circular opening, like a wedding ring, but wider than arms outstretched and deep enough to form a shallow tunnel. The rim was made of a solid silvery metal, like chrome steel, highly polished and with sharp, crisp edges. Inside was a second rim, an inner-ring made of hair-like copper wire wrapped round an iron core a million billion times to form a tight loop without beginning or end. Fine copper strands, like the veins in the white of an eye, periodically led from this inner core outwards, scribbling along the surface of the silver ring to a third, gold-coloured, ridge that ran around the outer circumference of the silver iris. Near the floor, this great ring had two thick, black cables connected to it that fell into a tangled mass, then snaked off, like roads, towards buzzing power-units under the stairs, and the computer at the distant end of the room.

This was a trans-dimensional portal: a machine that cuts a hole in time and space and even other universes, and allows a traveller to step through. It was a magic door, and George was going to use it to find a cure.

He stepped forwards, then stumbled to his knees as the left side of his head was sliced off. It felt like that. Searing pain. He saw red, and the sounds of the room faded into a deep hum layered on top with a high-pitched whine like a cake of agony. He passed out.

Chapter Three

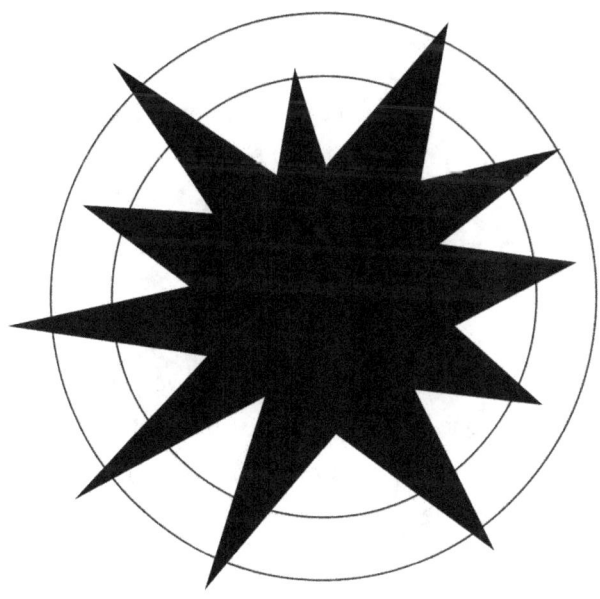

A blur of a moving person, coalescing into a twisting form. The tired face of a dark, straggle-haired woman in her fifties. A forgotten mother. She seemed to be searching for something, moving frantically around a house of white wood, opening drawers and cupboards. A red-haired blob was helping her, a man with indistinct features. The images faded into a dark smoke.

"Open your eyes," said a nasty voice. "Come on!"

A fist grabbed George by the hair, brown clumps of curl sprouting through the black-gloved fingers.

"Wakey wakey."

George squeezed out a startled "Agh!" and opened his eyes. He was sitting in an ancient wooden chair, carved and heavy like a dead king's throne. His arms were strapped in with thick brown leather belts, and his legs too, at the ankles. A blast of icy air hit his face. The room was small and octagonal; a stone chamber like a Gothic chapel. A curtain of thick crimson velvet was draped over a good part of the opposite wall, hung crudely on spikes. There was no door.

"That's better!" said the voice. A bony hand gripped George's shoulder tightly and a man stepped into view with the tap tap

tap of a firm knee-length boot. He was tall and thin, with grey features and black rings around his wide, pink eyes. He was dressed in a dark grey military uniform topped with a peaked officer's cap, black belt, and leather gloves. He was carrying a horse rider's whip and a sadist's expression.

"Good morning, Mister Vance. How nice of you to join us..." rolled the man's crisp syllables. He wheeled around the room arms wide, as if acting to an invisible audience of sky gods. "I'm afraid that you are quite stuck. Quite trapped. You are quite all mine!"

"Who are you?!" trembled George. He struggled against his bonds to prove his captor's point. "Where am I? Where's my wife??"

"Your wife!" snapped the interrogator "Your wife? She's with her friends, look!" With a flamboyant curl the man produced a crystal ball from his pocket and held it steady before George's gaze. The ball showed the sky's view of Pauline in their garden, keeling on the floor, in a ring of sunlight tending her sunflowers. George found the image uncommonly beautiful. He so wanted Pauline to turn around and look at him but she continued to work, humming to herself and whispering to the flowers.

"It's your fault she doesn't love you," said the interrogator softly. He took back the ball and whacked George's cold right hand with his whip. George winced and flexed his burning fingers.

"Let me go. There must be a mistake!" he whimpered.

"You've made the mistake!" The interrogator was an actor once more, the words now formed and spoken perfectly, vowels waltzing and consonants stabbing like psychotic daggers of sound. "Your life is a mistake. What a pathetic thing you are! Why can't you give her real children?" The interrogator was striding in squares with barely bending knees. He stopped: "Answer!"

"I... I'm infertile." George answered meekly.

The interrogator calmed down. "Your sexual failures are of only transient interest to me." He blinked slowly and turned to look at George, burning an x-ray gaze into his soul. His fingers danced with each other before him, hands twisting like living gears. They stopped. "You didn't really want a child, did you?"

George was suddenly in a sunny room, he had become a spectre near the ceiling in the corner of his childhood living room, gazing down at the scene below. He could see himself as a boy, playing on his own, making something from cardboard. Folding, glueing, with brown gummy glue in a plastic bottle. Chunks of coloured crayon were lying around. He was trying to get the pieces to stick but the glue wasn't strong enough. The cardboard kept bending outwards, springing open with great force as the frustrated child bent it into a curve, a cylinder. Pressing harder on the seams. Applying more glue, holding the body shut with both hands, waiting, hoping that it would fix. It was the body of a robot. He reached for an arm made from a thin cardboard tube. The body popped open once again. It was hopeless. George the child began to cry and look around the empty room. The scene faded.

The interrogator was staring right into George's face. He backed away and began to meander pensively around the room.

George looked down to the back of his hand and saw there the green lawn of his summer garden. Pauline was there, kneeling in the orb of light, hunched over and working. She was humming an old song, a few notes, it was *You Don't Bring Me Flowers*. Adam appeared and showed her something that he had found in the garden, George couldn't see what. Pauline sat up and smiled at the discovery. The scene faded, and George found himself looking at the back of his hand that once more rested on the arm of the wooden chair.

He took a deep breath in, closed his eyes and hung his head. A cool flow of air drifted across his face making his eyebrows flex like windswept palm trees. He opened his eyes and stared for an empty moment at the uneven cobbles of the floor. They were brightly lit with a pretty dancing glint. He raised his face and noticed two flaming torches on either side of the velvet curtain, stuck into rusty iron mounts that bled into the gritty stonework. The interrogator was pacing around, eyes down, touching his chin. George looked at him quietly for a few moments, then asked "Why am I here?"

"You are here to atone for your sins. You are soon to die and I'm here to help you confess."

The man seemed more reasonable now. Perhaps every dying person goes though this. Perhaps this oaken seat has seen many distinguished guests, great and small, in their last few weeks before the end. George stroked the wood with a curl of fingertips that ran from little to large, experiencing the delightful dull rapping sound and the soft-leather sensation of his finger pads on the smooth wood. He stopped his fingers and pressed into the warm oak, feeling each tiny channel and indentation, each river that grew and branched and faded away to gradual nothing. He looked down at the dark lines, each drawn by a fingertip, by a prisoner like him. Some lines proud and joyous. Some barely visible. Some neat, some crazy, going backwards and twisting in on themselves, but all recorded, all here, the tangible penance of the people who have been channelled through this ancient chair. He whispered to himself: "How many people have been here..?"

"Ah!" beamed the interrogator, suddenly gazing skywards like a girl recalling a first love, "Oh! I've killed so many brilliant people! Some were quite marvellous, and some, quite pitiful; the deaths I mean. I've killed small children who cried for their mothers. Mothers who cried for themselves. Soldiers, and clergymen. Murderers and kindly old gentlemen. Thieves, butchers, laundrette owners, policemen, whores. Writers. Readers. All dead. Some struggled. Some slept! Many confessed. Most. But not all..."

George noticed a tiny money spider near the bridged fingers of his hand, walking on the smooth dark parts of the ancient arm. It explored the place like an arachnid astronaut, loving each great step taken by each tapping leg. George could move a finger and crush it. He was suddenly aware that he had complete power over the life and death of the tiny helpless thing. In an instant his hand was flattened as the interrogator slapped his gloved palm onto George's fingers. The interrogator shone his wide, mad eyes, aiming to incite a furious response. George lifted his hand to see the spider's dead body, contorted into a ball of a flash of agony.

"Why?" said George, seething, staring directly at the interrogator.

The uniformed man was now holding a large butcher's knife, blade downwards. "No reason," he said bluntly, "I could have let the creature live. I could have killed it. I had no feeling either way. No malice. No mercy. It was a random act. I chose to kill it for no reason."

His face cracked into an evil grin, then with violence cried "Now I'm going to give you some of this!" and he stabbed the blade violently into the top left of George's skull. Agony. Blackness.

Chapter Four

George opened his eyes. He was lying in great comfort in his soft, wide bed, under the feather duvet that caressed him when his wife didn't. The bed was in the middle of a long wall, painted like the others in a flat lemon yellow that looked like it should smell of custard-cream biscuits. The door was closed and placed so that when the door was open Pauline could lie on her side and look into the hall. A dressing table stood opposite the bed, made of curls of white wood, and with a large oval mirror like something a silent film star might powder her face in front of. A cheap white television stood awkwardly on one corner, like an astronaut on guard in the palace of Versailles.

George blinked and enjoyed a deep breath. There was no pain. The thin yellow curtains floated towards him and the scent of summer met his nostrils. It was daytime.

He sat up and enjoyed the kingly feeling of lazing in bed. He caught a glance of his reflection in the oval mirror, a feeling he disliked. Often he would tweak the mirror a few degrees to one side to give him a preferred view of outside, a relaxing scene of gnarled sycamore branches that swayed back and forth.

This time he stared at himself. As he looked he saw Roger's face instead, and the rolling counterpane became a bright green lawn that breathed and glowed like the fresh smile of a baby. Tiny birds darted about the scene of spring, and copper butterflies chased around Roger's heroic torso in helical twists, then up to the rich plate of azure sky above. Roger grew stronger and younger with each pulsating breath. His arm was around Pauline's shoulder.

In a blink, the image was gone and George's grey face was back again. In front of the mirror, the wedding photo in its oval silver frame showed George, his arm was around Pauline's shoulder. The curtains blew a hello again and George turned to look at the clouds.

"I wonder what time it is?" he thought.

Beside the bed was a small cubical cabinet with a single drawer made of crisp pine wood. A large red telephone rested on top, with a notepad and thin gold metal pen, a tiny clock with glowing turquoise numbers, and a svelte silver lamp with a long neck like a sexy robot swan. George looked at the clock. It was six eleven. He found himself staring at the two little dots that separated the hours from the minutes. On. Off. On. Off. On. Off. Each second born with hope and optimism only to die and fade away, falling into the past like a man overboard, a stream of men overboard, each gripping their glowing turquoise life rings, gazing at the ever diminishing ship while

George, on deck, gazed back, unable to do anything but watch them sink into his memory and their oblivion.

George was suddenly aware that the ceiling light was on. It was pulsating gently in and out at a regular pace, and humming with a sound audible to an ear held close to the hot glass, a glass that smelled of fried dust and desert rocks. The light changed colour, drifting towards a dreadful flickering violet, then back to a warm yellow, then violet, then a beautiful green that cast out waves of relaxation and peace. A smell of warm summer grass filled the air. The curtains danced with a new gust of wind. The light outside was orange now, and beyond the thin pane was a flat land of green mosses and smooth lakes. Birds were singing their final praise to the day. An intense orange sun hung in the sky, touching a distant iron hill with its tip, dripping its heat and life onto the Earth below. The floor was a desert now. Fronds of tiny plants curled inwards and gripped a fist, rolling down and into the deep cracks in the baked plate ground. A white moon rose, stars rotating over the house and around, and clouds like laser streaks shot from horizon to horizon. Rain began to fall, a gentle scatter of droplets. A daisy, still open, shivered, and particles of desert dust bounced and rolled along the night floor, bounding into the sensitive white petals of the tiny flower. The air near the ground smelled of roses, and the desert became lush and rich again, still cast in the faint blue light of the three-quarter moon, now high and gazing down on the scene from a fantastic height. As new plants tumbled and spiralled, creaking out a new existence, the sun appeared once more, at first a slit of light and heat on the black obsidian horizon, then growing, glowing the sky red, then orange, then yellow, then violet. Yellow. Violet. Yellow. Flickering, strobing. On. Off. On. Off. On. Off.

The curtains blew into the room once more, waltzing graciously for one dramatic curl before being sucked back, pulled towards the window, covering it with their cotton film, showing each angle and sharp edge of the window frame. Marking the contours of the architecture like a brass rubbing that grasps at reality but never attains it. The light outside was now dim, and rain had begun to fall heavily, casting streaking shadows on the thin yellow drapes and hissing, dripping, making a periodic yet irregular tam tam tap sound on the glass of the open window, unseen.

The television fizzed into life. A war film was showing. Heroes were fighting in a castle and machine-gunning villains. Now villains were throwing grenades at heroes. A general stepped casually over the strewn corpses of a defeated foe. He was talking in an upper-class accent with a journalist about the progress of the war. A solider on fire ran screaming past the pair and was rifle-shot in the back. He fell face downwards out of sight and memory. The general lifted his gloved hand which was on fire. The pictures showed the brown leather glove, flickering, burning, immobile.

The ceiling light glowed zinc-blue.

The screen hissed a new image. It showed an actor playing the Roman emperor Augustus. He was still. His face fixed and staring. Dead. Immobile for minutes, hours, years. Dead.

George looked at the clock again. The two little dots of turquoise light were intensely bright, a light of supreme smallness and supreme power. Born. Died. Born. Died. Born. The seconds slowed down, filled with aeons of space. On. A spat of rain hit the window pane, sending filaments of water running like a hand grenade of panic. A startled fly looked up to see the gigantic grid of a swatter hurtling down upon it, cascading through the air in an arc of terror and hatred. A newborn chick gaped and screamed, its flapping mother arrived with a squirming worm. Adam was switched on for the first time. His circuits smelled of warm copper as his titanium irises slowly dilated into reflected consciousness. Kettles were boiled. Ships blessed, launched, retired, and sank. School bells rang. Adam, now rusty, tripped and fell down some stone steps with a clutter. His squeaking right hand grated as it feebly opened. Closed. Opened. Off. And the second fell away, the man in the life-ring drifting and falling away, beyond hope, beyond reach, lost forever. Lost. Gone. Gone!

The rain now sounded like a torrent. No light came from the curtains, just the dim ethereal glow of the ceiling light, pulsating and throbbing a mix of hues. Now the light seemed to be rotating, gazing around the room with a beam of intellect, searching for something. Seeking, scanning. The mirror on the bureau, the sexy lamp, the sunflower painting that hung over the bed, the crystal door knob, the telephone. The light lurched into a scarlet love-heart red, then spiralled like a hysterical lighthouse, shifting to orange, then yellow, then blue. Round and round. The moon was in the mirror, then the sun, then the moon. Day. Night. Day. Night. Day.

Lightning silently flashed, illuminating the sodden lemon curtains. The bulb cast a conical beam onto the clock, shining a bright-white light, like a projector in a smoky cinema. Inside the hot bulb, a trail of thought ran along the glowing filament, racing around the spiral within spiral, darting like a swarm of lightspeed rats, up and round, curling ever curling, charging, scraping and smashing along the tungsten track, bashing and bumping, making it glow white hot. As hot as the sun. Then, boom! Crash! The iron road ripped open, the tunnel torn apart, screaming like a china-plate dragon having its fingernails pulled out. The coils, broken, sprung apart, then bounced limply like an impotent slinky, hot, warm, cool, cold, black. Dead. The light went out. The room was black.

Terrified, George reached for the bedside lamp, fumbling for the switch. Click. Nothing. Click. Click. "Come on," he begged. "Please. Please! Somebody!"

The telephone rang its bell. Loud and imposing, the plastic body lighting up in hot red with each metallic scream. After a few rings George picked up the receiver: "Hello?"

A voice boomed: "This is God." Silence. A long silence.

"God?"

"This is God," repeated the voice.

George was an atheist. A scientist, and not remotely religious, except, that is, when times were very difficult. The times that deserved and benefited from an occasional prayer, or a beg to an unseen force. Those times when he needed a way to generate a fragment of peace, to grasp at rest or friendship by making a cold statement to somebody he could trust. Some imaginary body. At no point had George actually believed in the existence of a definite divine being, at least not since his childhood beliefs in Santa Claus or the Tooth Fairy. Now though, the time was right. Exactly right. Yes. This was God. This was exactly what George imagined God would be like, and exactly when he needed him, too.

"It's not fair," he said down the phone: "Why are you so cruel?" Pause. Nothing back.

"Why do you let some people have it all and take so much from me? What have I done? I've been kind. I have nothing..."

His eyes had become accustomed to the darkness now. A matrix of thin streaks of blue-grey moonbeams shone from the window. The rays lit up his wedding photo on the bureau opposite, the smiling face of a young Pauline when they were in love. Did she still love him? He didn't feel it. Was his lack of love for her the problem? He felt guilty and sad. At what point did their love stop? Could he unroll the past twelve years on a strip of paper and graph their love, blue pen for him, pink pen for her. Could he point to a day and say this was it, that argument about that bill or friend or television programme or other such pointless little thing.

Would she be sad when he died? Does she love Roger as much as he secretly hated him?

In the mirror George saw the sunflower painting, a

reproduction of the famous van Gogh painting in the National Gallery in London. It hung over the bed in a heavy gilt frame. The picture was an early birthday present for Pauline. The darkness concealed all but the most abstracted outlines, but the flowers stared out all the same, gazing and burning. Asking and listening.

"This is God."

The voice was a recording.

Chapter Five

George opened a crusty eyelid and flexed a stiff right hand. He was lying face down at the foot of the stairs in his laboratory. The computers were on. The humming florescent lights were flickering, making an irregular tapping sound. His head hurt. Blood was coming from his nostril. He wiped it with the middle finger of his hand and licked his lip. He sat up and stroked his hair into order. The lights strobed briefly and assumed luminous stability with a satisfying ping.

George creaked his stiff limbs into standing, then into moving to his soft leather office chair to relax and recover from his nightmare. He closed his eyes and massaged the nasion between, then clicked open a fresh bottle of mineral water from the top of his desk and took a sip.

George's desk was a kidney shaped aluminium slab, scattered with what looked like thousands of tiny squares of yellow paper, notes scribbled in blue pen with equations, drawings, shopping lists, to-do lists, names, numbers, everything imaginable. A rectangular flat screen protruded from the back of the desk on a sleek curving arm. The screen was casting a smooth blue light. A cursor there was slowly pulsing.

All of time and space was available. He could travel anywhere and anywhen, converse with the greatest minds in history... but where should he go and who should he see? What is his primary goal? Survival? Perhaps the first port of call should be someone who can advise him. Perhaps the wisest man in history... in all of time? Is there such a man?

The main computer was connected to a micro-atomic trans-dimensional conduit, a very tiny version of the great steel iris, a ring that was just large enough to transmit data back and forth electronically. This device acted like the small finder-scope on a telescope, detecting a destination before homing in with the main portal. A sophisticated artificially intelligent search algorithm was linked to this, allowing a particular person or place or event to be located based on specified criteria. News media, information networks, images, conversations; all of this could be scanned to locate the best match for a particular search request.

George touched the side of the computer screen with his right middle finger and a thin black keyboard slid out from a concealed recess. He pressed a red key and typed a few initial commands at speed, his face lit by the clean blue glow of the screen. He stabbed a final key, and a vast smash sound filled the basement, followed by a deep rumble as the gold outer ring of the main portal rotated slowly and locked into its active configuration.

He stood up and spoke: "Find the world's wisest man."

He was quite excited by this first real test. The red lights on the computer banks danced for a few seconds while it pondered this instruction.

"Located," said the cold voice.

"Open gateway," commanded George.

In the space within the great ring, tiny blue speckles began to glow into existence; floating loose in space, then pulled gently towards the circumference like drifting jellyfish, slowly turning, wheeling, coalescing into a spiral of light that gradually grew brighter and brighter, spinning faster and faster like a Catherine wheel. At different points along the rim the light reinforced, forming bright globules, like suns the size of ping-pong balls. At a certain critical moment these simultaneously exploded with an electric fizz, firing ultra-fine beams, like hairs of white light, across the plane of the disc at all angles, bouncing, reflecting, slicing the space inside the ring, criss-crossing the plane like a spider's web of increasing complexity, faster and faster, whiter and whiter until the disc became a solid face of hissing light, and then, in an instant, it faded to peaceful daylight. It showed the floor of a damp valley of grey rock. The ring had become a circular doorway.

"Gateway open," said the computer.

George stepped though. The clammy air smelled of mushrooms and charcoal, the cobwebs of autumn. The sky was grey, and shot with white streaks. The valley was slate and dreary, rising about a hundred feet on each side. Rough crags and rock falls led up the sides like natural steps, and despite the huge scale of the terrain it looked easily climbable. Weak trickles of water ran through cracks. Tough green grass stabbed though gaps in the rocks, and cascades of delicate ferns gripped soil and held on tight where they could. There were a few scrawny trees like sycamore with green shoots. It must have been sometime in early spring. The floor was sandy and glistening wet. It had been raining.

George looked behind him to see a disc in space. Beyond it was his basement laboratory. He could return at any moment. He started to explore, and looked around the back of his point of entry. The valley rose sharply and bent in a wall of shattered brown rock. He decided to walk forwards and followed what appeared to be a trail in the middle of the valley. Soon, the path veered to the side and began to climb the mountain, hugging the wall on a crunching, rocky path only a few feet wide. The sheer wall on the side suddenly fell away and revealed a beautiful clearing of short green grass, that bordered a small lake of black water fed by a crackling waterfall. The water sprayed a fresh forest scent as it cascaded into a miasma of foam.

He stepped cautiously onto the fresh grass and moved towards the edge of the lake, and at that point he noticed a thin man, wearing a brown sheet and a grey beard, sitting perfectly still on a flat rock only a few feet away. The man had his eyes closed. He opened them, looked straight at George, and deftly leapt down to stand before him.

"Hello friend," he said in a rich, round voice. He clasped his rubbing hands together near to his shoulder and screwed an eye closed, using the other to peer at George with a grin: "You don't look dressed for the mountains."

He stroked his fingers through his bedraggled facial hair. He had circular, gold-rimmed spectacles that windowed muddy brown eyes of about fifty years. His skin looked soft, and was finely spattered with grey mud and patches of the redness that accompany an outdoor life. On his shoulders hung a loose dress, like a monk's cassock, tied at the waist with a silk scarf twisted with rainbow colours. His distant hairline led to a river of grey hair with black streaks, pulled neatly into a ponytail and greased with an oil that didn't look artificial.

"Um, no..." said George with a slight smile that acknowledged the joke "I've come a long way to see you. I'm George." He extended a hand. The man took it with coarse, earthy digits. "I'm Meeter McKreet." He smiled with a cheery glint in gappy yellow teeth, then he gave George an unexpected hug, patting his shoulder as he pulled away. Meeter smelled of smoke. "Come on in! We're all friends here," he said with a mischievous wink.

Meeter turned and began to shuffle away, hobbling and creeping up a staircase of smooth rocks and watery moss in his bare feet, traversing a well-trodden yet invisible path. George followed as best he could, awkwardly picking his way in his leather shoes and office trousers, the lower half of which had already been autographed by the local clay.

Meeter slipped into a cave, startlingly high up in the middle of the shattered wall that George had walked beside. George followed him into echoing darkness. The cave entrance looked out onto the lake, giving an impressive view of the distant waterfall on the opposite side, the sound which now rattled in every direction. On the floor a trail of rusty rock bled forth like a red carpet. In it, near the gaping entrance someone had carved the letters AEAEA. In the blackness ahead George could perceive a dim glow. He moved cautiously forwards, around a twisting corner and then stepped into a fabulous cavern of golden light and unexpected warmth.

The huge cave was teeming with children of all ages. Near one wall was a battered leather sofa, once all brown and now spidered with the grey of age. Three women shared it: a young, fair skinned woman with streaming flat hair, wearing something like a toga, and a vacant expression. Next to her a plump woman, breast exposed and suckling an infant; and last, an olive-skinned woman of middle age and uncommon beauty, with crisps of jet-black hair and black eyes like the depths of outer space if it were liquid.

The middle of the floor was covered in a shaggy grey animal fur. Ovoid electric lights hung from the ceiling over metal hooks that were hammered into the rock, their snaking cables running through a dark doorway at the end of the huge back wall. That wall was covered with paintings of all sorts, some framed, many on driftwood or angular bits of paper. Some drawings of faces and nudes were scrawled onto the wall directly, in charcoal or chalk. Some were crudely fashioned. Some were very good. A cluster of children were scribbling there with crayons.

There was a huge concert-grand piano, battered and scarred, muddied, and criss crossed with years of accidental abuse and deliberate graffiti. Occasional glimpses of its once polished black perfection blinked meekly out. Next to it was a drum kit, skins plastered with black tape, and on the floor a red electric guitar, wired into a dented black amplifier. Along the wall, behind the instruments, were books piled high in toppling stacks. Some on bamboo shelves, many on the floor, higgledy piggledy, the stochastic arrangement of a gaggle of uncaring librarians.

Some young ragged children were noisily running in figure eights around the musical instruments. George noticed something in the corner of his eye and looked down to see a boy of about sixteen lying flat in a star shape, eyes closed, two fingers of his hand loosely holding a cigarette that released a thin stream of sweet smelling smoke. Behind him, in deep shadows, were the huddled naked legs of an unmoving girl of the same age, maybe older. An empty syringe lay on the floor.

"Come in!" invited Meeter, up ahead. "Sit down." Meeter crouched in the middle of the rug and lay on one side like a casual Roman Emperor.

George felt uneasy.

A small dirty child appeared and said: "Who are you?"

"I'm George," he said, and the children began to chant his name as they ran around in circles. The plump woman stabbed out a command to try and make them stop.

George winced. A gulp of pain burst behind his eye and ran

into the depths of his head. Meeter detected it. "What's up, mate? Come on, sit down."

George stepped in and sat on the floor before Meeter, leaning on his palm. For a cave, the room was surprisingly comfortable. George clutched a fist of his thick hair. His head pain abated.

"I've got a headache," he said. "Actually, it's worse than that. A terminal brain tumour. I'll be dead in a few weeks and I wanted to ask your advice."

"Would you like to have sex with my wife?" blinked Meeter. The olive skinned woman cast her eyes to the sky in exasperation. George didn't expect he meant her.

An embarrassed George stammered, "Um, no."

"Are you sure? She wouldn't mind."

"No, it's okay. I'm married."

"That would be my advice," said Meeter abruptly. "What does it matter if you're married, you're going to be dead soon, so you said. You should make the most of the time you've got left."

George began to think. A shorter lifespan doesn't mean that the way you live should change. The right way to live, the right thing to do, should be the same whether you had a year to live, or ten years, or ten days. If you knew you had an hour to live, maybe you could go crazy on some sort of lawless rampage, just for fun or some visceral animal pleasure... but why? There would always be consequences, for others if not for you; and besides, nobody knows exactly how long they will live anyway, unless they had a suicide plan and a supreme amount of discipline. That would be insane.

Meeter was waiting patiently for a response. George caught a glimpse of Meeter's wrist and saw upon it some numbers in blue ink... a concentration camp tattoo?

Meeter spoke up: "Do you wanna drink then?" He rolled to his side and grabbed an unmarked bottle of clear liquid from next to the sofa, before deftly rolling back into crossed legs. "I make it myself." He unscrewed it and poked the bottle under George's nose. George pulled away at the eye-watering fumes.

"Good stuff, eh?" cackled Meeter. He took a swig and smacked his gooey lips before wiping the neck with his forearm.

A crackle of headache exploded in George like a blooming flower. He stood up.

"Is there a toilet nearby?" he asked.

"Sure, mate, through there," said a gently gyrating Meeter. He waved a hand towards the black hole at the back. A small girl wobbled up to Meeter holding a cloth bag, picking at the zip. "Carn open it," she said at him. Meeter took it gently and began to wrestle with the fastener. George crossed the busy room, past the piano and through the doorway.

He was in a small cold chamber. A doorway in the corner led to another space, and in the wall ahead a square of sky at head height lit the room, making his surroundings a warm orange. The sun was setting. The puckering hum of a petrol generator touched his ears, its acrid blue smoke mixed with the sewage smell that floated up from a hole in the slate floor. He relieved himself down the hole. On the wall before his gaze was a framed photograph of Meeter, neatly groomed and dressed in a dark suit. He was posed next to another smart looking man and clutching a golden trophy. A caption said "Professor Meeter McKreet B.A. B.Phil. Ph.D."

How could such a clever man end up here, a bedraggled drunk, a pot head, good for nobody? What was the use of a wise man who kept his wisdom to himself?

George poked his head through the window and saw a vista of

bleak, rolling hills before a setting sun of hot lava hues and pink flights of cloud. Below him, layers of cracked rock fragmented in wide shards. A trickle of polluted water flowed from his cave, vomiting through the cracks and into a wide grey gyre of congealed mess on a large pool. Mountains of debris, like unlit bonfires, sat next to it: a rusted bed and a rotten mattress, black metal boxes of dead electronics, soiled clothes, sodden cardboard, and flakes of plastic which coughed in the fresh wind. George shivered.

He pulled his head back and noticed a boy in the adjoining room, his outline lit by the coppery glow of the setting sun. The boy was twelve or thirteen and sitting in silence, looking out over an expansive arched window that led to a makeshift balcony facing west.

"Hello," said George, ambling in to sit by the boy.

The boy flashed a smile but said nothing. Then, after a pause: "Where are you from? The city?"

"Yes, in a way," said George.

"I want to go there," said the boy, still looking at the sky, "I want to go to school. They just mess around all day. I hate it here." He stood up and moved towards the wide window that filled the wall.

George looked around the boy's room. A low, neat bed lay in the shadow of the distant corner. There were toys and comics on the stone floor, and a raffia mat in the middle. Posters were peeling from the wall beside the bed. One was of a young woman with olive skin, the Latino woman from the main cave as she was years ago. The poster advertised a piano concert, a performance of Rachmaninov's Piano Concerto No. 2 by Maria Andrade the "Great Brazilian Concert Pianist". George recognised the name; of course! In George's home, an old recording of Maria's was resting askance on a beechwood shelf in his front room. Her music was filled with emotion and deep meaning, so brilliantly expressed, as though the very softness of each gentle push of each key pressed against ones abdomen, along the naked back of each listener. Yet played by a girl of just seventeen, one plucked from a darker quarter of a tumbling Brazilian city.

"Your mother..?" asked George.

"Yes," said the boy. "When she was young."

"Does she still play?"

"Sometimes."

"Do you?"

"Yes. Would you like to hear me play?" The boy became enthused by this. The pair walked back to the lit cave and the noise and tumult. The boy ignored everyone and pulled a small piano stool out from underneath the great instrument. Up close, this furniture looked grand indeed, no longer an abused wreck, but an aged butler, peacefully and silently tolerating each mark and scar, standing upright in quiet, proud dignity.

The boy raised the lid and began to play. At first a slow chord, the piano out of tune, and then stroking the keys, darting fingers and arching wrists with deft flair. The tuning of the instrument was bad. The chords were discordant and notes hummed and jarred against each other as the sound waves clashed, yet, his hands flowed beautifully, with such grace and perfection, racing to the extremes of the keyboard at speed and yet pressing and caressing each note as though kissing each string slowly. The sad voice of the piano was an insult to his brilliance. George touched his shoulder and he stopped, looking up.

"Amazing," said George. "You're really good."

The lid was closed by Maria, suddenly standing at the end of the keyboard.

"We only play for fun," she snapped in a strong accent. Her voice seemed angry, yet, in the vast black pools of her eyes, George saw the most immense sadness. The anguish of a genius trapped in a dark cell.

"This place is not fun!" cried the boy. He stood, shoving the piano stool angrily backwards and striding towards his room, towards a secret curl of rope beneath his bed, his wide window, and his eventual escape.

"He was right," thought George. The piano being new and in tune wouldn't make this empty place any better. A life of meaningless pleasure only makes that meaninglessness more apparent. That boy was the only wise person here.

"I will go," said George to Maria, then a polite goodbye to the now oblivious Professor McKreet. He strode along the rug, looking straight ahead, and into the passage to see and hear the magnificent tumble of white water, then creeping down the irregular stones like a careful crab, to the beautiful green bed, the clean newness that carpeted the fringes of the entrance to this cold paradise.

He turned, keeping the wall on his opposite side this time, and faced the last segment of the setting sun, its crimson touch was now illuminating the tips of the splintered rock around him; a glitter of goodbye. Soon he saw the disc-shaped hole in space, the perfect circle that led back home. He shivered in the evening chill, glad to see his laboratory, something warm and dry and familiar. He walked though and wearily said: "Close gateway."

Chapter Six

George felt good to be in the comfortable order of the laboratory. Behind him, there was a silent white flash, and the magic portal became once more a hollow empty ring. He found himself squeezing one eye closed. The pain had stopped although he felt an uncomfortable heaviness there, as though part of his head had been transformed into putty. Perhaps it was psychological. Perhaps the absence of pain with the knowledge of it returning was worse than the pain itself.

His stomach gurgled. He moved over to a radiator and bathed his icy hands in the warm rolling air that soared above it. It felt heavenly.

Heaven. Surely an actual paradise would be free of the worries that limit a human domain. Could such a place exist, some paradise among the dimensions? A happy place where the just and kind among the dead reside? Could each of us contain some part that works like the portal machine, a sparkling fragment of brain, the seed of a seed that marks out the original location of the single cell that divided and divided and divided to eventually become ourselves? Perhaps he could ask the computer to search now, just to see what would happen.

"Find heaven."

The tiny red lights on the main computer towers flickered as database correlated with database, thought tracked thought, and every experience in time and space and the detectable universe was scanned, probed, cross-referenced and indexed. Every feeling could be tested. Every combination of neurotransmitter and electric circuit prodded. Every news report, anecdote, medical record, theological debate. Every tear from every dying solder or saint. Every plea from each victim. Each echo of every prayer. Every arrangement of every particle, from the iron ice inside a black hole to the final thin breath of an extinct universe at the supra-ultimate border of time itself.

The dots flickered with an increasing urgency, then at an alarming speed. Suddenly the ceiling lights went out and the hum of the machinery became a whine, and the whine a staircase of sound, ever climbing, beyond the range of human ears, of dogs, of tiny rodents, of startled ants, surprised fleas, bed bugs, viruses, and angels. A silver pen began to rattle on the aluminium desk, and the carpet of tiny papers began to shift and glide on its surface as the room first shivered, and then quivered, and then quaked, as though the whole world had become anxious at the prospect of meeting the creator of all things. George, agape, gripped the back of his shuffling chair, ready to voice the abort command; but not quite yet. Not until the search was complete. Not unless things became very dangerous.

Then, in an unexpected instant, all was calm. The ceiling lights glowed and bounced back into life. The pen breathed a sigh of relief. A single square of paper slid off the table like a prisoner given permission to jump, and it glided in arcs of zigs and zags until its edge hit the ground with a gentle smack.

"Located," said the computer with no emotion.

George's stomach grumbled. If there was a heaven, there would be food. Even if there was no food he had to see what the computer had found. He had to at least look.

"Open gateway," he instructed nervously. He stood back from the gate and wondered if he should bow down, or cower, or perhaps simply hide behind something? The web was building. The disc was white. The gate opened.

The first thing George noticed was a beautiful smell, like red rose petals' breath over soft young skin. A wave of it flowed from the portal like invisible hair, romancing and enticing every nostril in range. The breeze itself felt like warm air on a cold day, or cold air on a hot day, and tasted of newborn mountain oxygen. The view was of a well kept English garden. A field of bright green grass, as smooth as that on a bowling green, extended for what seemed like miles. Rolling hills defined the distant horizon, some topped with forests, some with purple mountains. On some he could just make out structures of white marble in a pure geometric style. The sky was azure. It looked like the first real day of spring. An invisible intangible cord of love pulled him mesmerically towards the gate, and he stepped though.

The field was spread out before him like a blanket. It seemed vast in each direction, but gently rolled downwards, mimicking the topology of the distant hills. Occasional twisted fruit trees peppered the landscape to the right, and a small, well lit, wooded area lay behind the portal. There were some people too, too far to be in earshot. Some running or playing like children, and some resting and talking. They all looked young, and wore thin white clothes, like night dresses, that draped like translucent snowdrops, swaying and flowing in the gentle breeze. In the clear sky George noticed a yellow dot, like a silent aircraft, moving towards him at speed. It was a person, but something beyond human, something different and beautiful that had choral music attached, a melody that sang in smooth flows like the snakelike movements of its long white-gold hair.

It landed before George and folded its wings of golden feathers. Without the wings, the powerful creature looked human; about seven feet tall and almost beyond gender, but perhaps more female, with a smooth skin and small breasts.

The pubic regions were enigmatic, swathed in diaphanous drapery like a Greek god in a Botticelli painting. Her irises were gold, and as deep as a dark sun. About her forehead, binding her long loose hair, was a smooth gold circlet. A voice like white light in a black room spoke: "Welcome, sir. You are loved by the Master. I am Zarnael, twenty-nine nine of the house of Raptallion. I will take you to your family."

"My family?" thought George, too awed to speak, "...but they're all at home!" He hadn't remotely thought that his dead relatives might be here. What an unexpected situation. He might meet his father again. "This is amazing!" he said. Zarnael smiled gently, her kind face expressing the feelings of a research professor amused by a particularly adept mouse.

"Come," Zarnael said.

She extended a hand and George instinctively moved to shake it. When skin touched skin he found himself flying at a vast and immeasurable speed; over fields, forests, oceans, through clouds of white warmness and wet fogness, all a blur, all an instant, and yet seeming to feel and see every event, location, sensation. Suddenly he was standing again, but in a new place. Zarnael drew back her hand and nodded towards a pool of grass behind George's shoulder. George turned, and there, leaning back, eyes closed, in the shade under a blossoming apple tree, was his long-dead father, Rothko Vance.

George gaped and looked around. This garden was small, and felt comfortable and homely, like the country garden of his childhood home. There were rose bushes and lots of well tended flowers, friendly fruit trees, paths made of yellow gravel and others of moss. There were marble statues, like those of Greek antiquity, and abstract bronzes that could have come from the early twentieth century. A silver sundial on a plinth occupied in the centre of the circular lawn that he and Zarnael stood upon. There were quite a few people here, all dressed in the limp, flowing gowns. Most were sitting or lying around, resting or asleep. Some were talking quietly. There were some children chasing each other. All were youthful and beautiful. None were touching each other.

Zarnael spoke, staring through George to infinite distance: "This is one of our gardens. We have many, and many, and many. You can have anything you desire. All you need to do is will it. The Master will provide."

"All I have to do is will it?" mouthed George. He put out his hand and thought: "Wine."

Nothing happened. He tried again: "WINE!" More insistently, shaking his hand as though striking an invisible bell with an invisible stick. Still nothing.

"You must imagine the essence of what you desire," spoke Zarnael. "Feel it. Picture it. Smell it. Use every sense, but especially its essence, its feeling to you." George tried again and a champagne flute appeared, filled with chilled sparkling wine. He smelled its acidity, then tasted it and licked his lips. It was perfect. He then noticed for the first time that he felt no hunger. His head didn't hurt either, but it didn't feel exactly different.

He sipped the champagne. Zarnael spoke: "You may speak to your father. I will remain here." She folded her arms and stared straight ahead with a neutral expression. Rothko had died of lung cancer when George was seventeen. He was over forty when he fathered George, a workaholic and not an agile man. He didn't play much with his son but each moment was precious. Rothko's young death affected George deeply, and George idolised his memory.

George walked over to his father. He looked young, much younger than George, perhaps nineteen, and had short black hair slicked back like a nineteen-fifties rebel. One leg was up, supporting a sleepy arm. He held a sweet smelling cigarette between two fingers. His eyes were closed.

"Dad..."

Rothko opened his eyes like a man with a hangover and lifted his head. He squinted, straining, confused. George continued: "It's me, George."

"George? George, my boy. Yeah, I remember you."

Some dark recess in Rothko's mind had awakened a memory of a past life. George didn't know what to say. He was suddenly overcome with emotion but couldn't quite say why. He took a gulp of champagne and blinked to conceal his tears. In the space between George and Rothko, a large, bright blue butterfly flew. It smelled of sweet vanilla, and gently circled its wide wings, casting tiny iridescent particles into the air, each speck turning in a delicate spiral. George tracked the flight of this fabulous creature as he wiped his eyes dry.

"This place is beautiful," he sniffed.

"Yes, it's perfect here. Every day starts and ends with angelic music. The nights are never too cold and the days are never too hot. We can eat and not get fat. We can smoke." He flashed a smile at a hidden joke, then closed his eyes and took a drag, blowing aromatic smoke with the least possible effort. "We don't need to work, or eat, or do anything. We can pretty much do what we like. Every day. Forever." He exhaled a laugh through his nose at the joke again and dragged on his cigarette. The laugh was the most he'd moved since the conversation began.

George finished off his champagne. He didn't feel remotely drunk. Actually, not even a tiny bit, not even a fragment of a fragment of drunkenness. He wrinkled his brow. "This seems an odd thing to ask but, can we get drunk here?"

A sudden cold wind blasted George, rattling some leaves along the way. Rothko smiled again, keeping his eyes closed and took another lazy drag. There was a long pause. "No. Do you think drunks would improve the place?" Rothko let out a laugh. "Maybe they would."

Another gust of wind magically appeared, throwing a handful of dust towards Rothko.

"Alright alright," said Rothko, half asleep and not really caring. George wondered who he was talking to. He looked around, then turned and plopped down under the tree next to his dad. There were nine or ten people in sight. He looked at a few, wondering if any more relatives were here. He didn't know much about his family, not the dead ones anyway, but he'd probably recognise his dad's parents and his old uncle George, the man he was named after. He was struck by the small blond boy running around the sundial. He looked remarkably like George himself when he was young. He had to be a relative. Perhaps people here could choose their age. Perhaps he was uncle George!

"Hey!" he called. "Hey!" The boy heard and came closer. "Who are you? What's your name?"

The boy squatted down cross legged and gazed at George with a wide blue-eyed smile. "My name's Adam. Who are you?"

"Adam? That's my son's..." Then George stopped.

"He's my grandson," grated Rothko, opening his eyes. "You should have had him and got him out of this place." George was confused. Rothko elucidated. "You don't have to die to come here. Everyone who hasn't been born yet is here too. He's the son you didn't have. The children are the unborn ones. The adults are the dead ones."

"Are you my father?" said Adam excitedly, then: "Why are you old?"

"I'm old because I'm just a visitor here, I came from my home with a machine that I invented. I'm still alive."

"Can I come back with you? It's so boring here!"

"Well..."

"Please!"

George hadn't thought of that. He suddenly pictured the hole in space on that heavenly field. What if some curious spirit wandered through it and into his basement? Could he take friends back? Could he take his father? His son? Zarnael answered these questions with an unquestionable voice: "It is not permitted."

Rothko burst a laugh, coughing out a glob of smoke and jerking like a puppet on rubber string. He took another drag. George was sure his cigarette was the same length as ever. "Aww," moaned Adam. "Tell me about the Earth. I love the Earth. I so want to be alive! What it's like to be hungry?"

Behind Adam, Zarnael raised an attentive eyebrow.

"Hungry?" mused George. "Hmm, it's quite difficult to explain to someone who has never experienced it... well... it's not very nice, sort of like a hollow, cold feeling that grows more hollow and cold. Eventually your stomach hurts and makes noises, and you feel tired and weak... but when you eat you feel better, and warm again."

Adam looked confused. "You mean cold inside like when you're all alone on an island... and then you're forgiven and taken back!?"

"Not really... It's not really like loneliness." George paused. What a strange comparison for Adam to make. Had this child read Robinson Crusoe? Or heard about islands from the other people here? Or... been sent to an island as some sort of punishment? He caught the eyes of Zarnael while thinking and the glance of the powerful creature seemed to be probing him. It made George nervous. He looked at the floor, the sky, the sundial. He returned to the subject of the conversation.

"Hunger is not nice. You're lucky not to feel it." Then George paused again. That champagne didn't affect him at all. If you didn't need food and never got hungry then the primary pleasure of eating wasn't there. Without hunger, food would be pointless. At best a taste without the desire, salivation without the warm glow of satiation. Perhaps a taste of food without those things would be like the meaningless and inconsequential touch of clothing against the skin. He looked down at his right arm, suddenly aware of each brush of fabric against it. He noticed that he was wearing one of the gossamer gowns that everyone else was wearing. That was odd. It must have happened during his flight. He suddenly felt self-conscious. This was the third or fourth time George had felt uncomfortable here and he didn't like it. Everything looked and felt beautiful, but the eternal smiles of the lazing populace seemed somehow false. What wasn't he being told?

Adam flopped onto his back, staring into the endless sky and twisting his tentacular arms in eternal fidget. "I think Earth is brilliant!"

"What's so good about Earth?" queried George. "Trust, me it's not perfect. I'm guessing that a perfect place like this could be boring, perhaps that's why people seem a little different here, but time is yours to fill, and, I suppose Heaven isn't like Earth so the people are bound to be different."

"Boring!?" exclaimed Rothko. He jumped up, at last animated. "Oh, it's not that!"

"Silence." commanded Zarnael. She unfolded her arms. "Philosophical discussions are not permitted!"

A blast of wind appeared, making the leaves shiver and fizz. The last few people in the garden crept nervously out of sight leaving the four alone on the island of grass. George was taken aback. Rothko sat back down and hung his head in submission.

He took a drag and mumbled something under his breath. Adam looked terrified, his tiny body crunched into a ball with his eyes tightly clenched. Philosophical discussions banned? Was this not Heaven? Surely all of the greatest philosophers are here, somewhere? Zarnael tried to calm the situation and softened her voice: "Do not be afraid. We must have rules to keep order. Every society needs government, the alternative is anarchy."

"Rules?" said George. "How many rules are there?"

"This place is full of rules," laughed Rothko. He burst out laughing and launched his cigarette into the air. It landed on the grass, still smoking. Now Zarnael looked worried.

"There, I just broke one!" said Rothko defiantly.

The eternally summer sky had darkened and shifted almost imperceptibly towards green. At a distant point, a slice on the rim of the north-east horizon, there was a tiny flash, unseen by all. It began to carve a black crack that crept upwards. The branches of the trees were creaking and stretching, curling away and inwards. Little flurries of wind were tossing handfuls of soil and loose grass around. A butterfly on the polished sundial fluttered manically, clattering its wings on the gnomon and making a sound like a boy running a stick in the spokes of a spinning wheel. Everyone stayed silent. Zarnael was unsure what to do, eventually electing to talk and calm the situation. The air of ultra-superiority that she had initially held in George's mind had partly fallen away. "Our society is perfect. We only want the best for the population. Rules are necessary because to be completely free would quickly impinge on another being's freedom..."

"What about when you're alone?" interrupted George.

"Even when alone, your living cells have rights. They deserve not to be injured by your free choices." said Zarnael, confident in her argument.

The sky was now quite dark and the air chilly. Its blue had become an insipid green. A thin streak of violet-black clouds was now clearly visible, moving across the dome of the sky and towards the garden, a pointed finger flying towards the four at the speed of sound. Zarnael spread the fingers of her hand and held her arm aloft, towards the approaching storm. It seemed to be a signal that all was under control. Adam suddenly jumped up and ran, darting away behind the cowering trees and beyond. Zarnael let him go.

"We're in the shit now!" giggled Rothko looking skyward. He laughed like a psychotic driver in a terminal game of chicken.

Zarnael continued at a frenetic pace, desperately trying to regain control of the situation. She grasped at words that fell like a house of tumbling cards. Order had to be restored.

"We cannot all be free and all be happy; the two are incompatible... so happiness was chosen. And we are happy. We can all be happy, if we follow the rules."

George couldn't find fault with the logic. Even a perfect society had to be a mix of people that had to get along with each other. If one person wanted to harm another, just for fun, it couldn't be allowed, so there had to be some sort of legal system, and some sort of penal system too, even in Heaven. The only alternative would be forbidding free thought. George remembered the false smiles on the people in the garden, like the senseless grin of an old woman with Alzheimer's disease. Rothko seemed able to think, and rebel, though. As did Zarnael. Even in a hierarchy the upper echelons would have to abide by rules for the same reasons, to preserve order.

The cards were now at rest. Not in a perfect house, not stacked in an ideal way, but stable. Zarnael exhaled and folded her arms. She then stared at Rothko, transmitting a message they both understood, and a few seconds later George's father picked up the cigarette, then took a drag, all the time wide eyed at Zarnael. He blew a stream of smoke in her direction, a last symbolic act of defiance, then laughed to himself. Something bothered George though. He had one more thing to ask.

"Who makes the rules?"

"He does!" shouted Rothko, pointing up. A column of black smoke was flying down, shooting towards the garden, turning and swirling like death and thunder. A cyclone of fury with an eye of green light was about to crash. The air was roaring.

"We all..." Zarnael shouted over the roar. She had to grasp at the cards. She had to regain control; "We ALL..."

Lightning exploded beside Zarnael, screaming with ten thousand degrees of heat and a sound like a train-wreck being tortured. Everyone was knocked off their feet. There was smoke, and soil, and leaves, and sharp bits of bark everywhere. The garden smelled of oak-smoked cordite. When the smoke cleared two creatures were flanking Zarnael, altogether different from the angelic being that welcomed George. These stood about nine feet high and had grey skin, four arms, and muscles like Heracles' slightly stronger best friend. They wore breastplates of a solid, silver-blue metal that hung from their enormous shoulders on great chains. Thick, knee and elbow pads had big spikes in the middle made from the same metal.

On their hips they wore a short skirt, made from red leathery straps and held up with a belt; its silver buckle embossed with the symbol of a lightning bolt. Their wide eyes were of solid gold, and they had white beards of straight, flat hair. Two thin horns, like those of an antelope, protruded from their foreheads making a vee.

"Philosophical discussions are not permitted!" one boomed. "Zarnael twenty-nine nine you will be punished according to chapter eight of the constitution."

Zarnael bowed to him and knelt on one knee. "I plead guilty. I submit." She spread both arms wide, palms downward.

George was on the floor. He had been knocked backwards, and the tree he had been under was now in front of him. His hands were scratched, his head throbbing. So much for a Heaven without pain.

"Fsst!" It was Rothko, now crouched behind him. "Come on dude we've gotta go."

"Wha..." uttered George.

"Now! Come on!"

The head of one of the great beasts turned to focus upon George. A grey muscular arm was extended. George staggered back on his kicking feet, then stood, turned, and ran away as fast as he could. The trees seemed to blur and shoot past. Objects in front of him seemed to fall behind in a curiously magical way as he darted through the heavenly landscape. He caught a glimpse of Rothko who was running too. George put out an arm and he felt as though he were flying forwards, a metre or so above the undulating terrain, then he panicked, tripped, and rolled his bony back over some hard sticks, crashing through a bush in a daze. He froze in the undergrowth, panting, terrified. A few seconds later Rothko poked his head in. "This is fun!" he wheezed with a grin. "He can see us, even read our thoughts, but He can't make us think what He wants! Even He has rules!"

Above the bush, dark clouds were massing, swirling and boiling. The horned creatures were not running but stomping, with infinite and justifiable confidence towards George and Rothko.

"Let's get out!" said George; his nose was now bleeding. "I arrived in the middle a field, a vast grassy plain, any idea where that is? How we can get there? There has to be some escape?"

Rothko snapped his fingers. "Out. Now that's somewhere nobody's been before. I know the place. Do you know how to fly?"

"Fly?"

"Yep, just think it and we'll go. Come on!"

Rothko jumped and flew off, pausing a few metres off the ground to turn and beckon George, who ran instead, through the bush, over a stream, left, right, past a tree, and jumped. Rothko was just in front, and George looked up. He darted right, around the boulder, stepped onto a rock, then leapt. There was a splash. Behind him, the two horned creatures were running too. They sensed George's plan, his optimism, his dreams of escape. They could feel his hope, and he, their threat. George flowed over the terrain like liquid fog, at first slow, then faster, like a steam-train caterpillar, bending, swerving. He pushed past a tree which had spikes on its bark and cut his hand. No time to stop. He ran on, frantic, sensing the hot breath of the grey beasts on the skin of his neck. The monsters split; one leapt and became airborne, chasing down Rothko, streaking through the sky like a grey homing-missile.

The terrain was becoming increasingly rough, and streams and gullies of rocks seemed to be appearing, trees and grass falling behind. George was taking risks, hopping at an insane speed from angled boulder to jagged rock. Slipping over wet, black stones, and splashing through water that was getting too deep to run though. Behind him, the beast was gaining on him. Each splash of George was heard again a few seconds later. Suddenly the floor fell away, and George skidded to a stop on the edge of a mountain precipice. He glanced up to the sun, just in time to see Rothko grabbed by the flying beast. Rothko's arms pushing and struggling against the iron grip of the four armed creature. Then, in the distance, he saw it. Below him, many miles away, a pure-white circle that looked like a dinner plate floating above a tablecloth of green fields. This was his gateway, his exit and way out of this place. The branches behind him cracked as his pursuer approached. He was seconds away from capture. He had no choice, his only option was to try and fly, so he quickly summoned every particle of hope, and jumped.

And he fell. Down. His fear dragged him, and the more he grasped at the sky, the greater his fear of falling grew and the faster he fell. Past the mountainside and down, tumbling towards the deadly rocks below. All he could see was where he should be. His head felt like a balloon, the side of face swollen and in pain. He gripped his face and closed his eyes tightly.

Suddenly he felt arms around him. He was no longer falling

and his fear had instantly vanished to become hope, love, something wonderful. He opened his eyes and saw Zarnael carrying him. They were flying towards the portal like a beam of sound, flashing over the great distance, over the spring fields to safety. The pair landed in front of the gate.

"T-Thankyou!" beamed George.

"When you come here again, things will be different." said Zarnael, smiling back. She turned and looked towards the approaching finger of storm: "Now, go!"

"Come with me!" said George.

Zarnael laughed. "This is my home. Do not worry. I will be alright."

There was a cracking sound in the air and Zarnael bent forwards. Her head began to swell, and her limbs became thinner, then greener. A white thorn burst through her arm, and then another through her side, and a third from her ear. Now a vibrant, crimson collar appeared and grew huge, eventually wrapping her head in a spiral of soft petals. Within seconds she had transformed into a red rose. Her delicate petals quivered in the soft air that flowed from the summer fields.

George looked to the sky. An arm of cloud was approaching, but now he knew he was safe. He jogged through the gateway that led back to his home and gave the command: "Close gateway," and everything was quiet, and calm, and safe, and homely.

He blew a thankful breath into space and flexed the fingers of his grazed hand. A lone note was lying discarded on the floor and George picked it up, touching the yellow paper to his lips.

He was home. Was that place real? Was it a dream? Was that really heaven, or another place, somewhere in the vast universe where beings live and die like anywhere else? He thought about Rothko, the father he wanted to know, and the teenager full of life and greatness that he always knew and hoped his father would be.

He put the paper on the desk and slumped into his office chair. The leather was soft, and its forms moulded just for him. He felt no pain, only a reflective contentment. He was ready to relax, sleep and rest. Then he glanced at the computer clock, no, surely that can't be right? The date? Two weeks had passed since he had entered the gate! He became alert again, frantic, and typed a few commands. The date appeared correct. He checked the gate logs. It was true. Then a stabbing pain struck his head. His time was fizzing away. How could he be so stupid!? How could he let time slip through his fingers like sand in an hourglass!? Precious seconds. Precious minutes! Each gone forever, floating in the turquoise sea. Lost. Lost!

He had to find a cure, he just had to. Just a short time to work and then he could rest. Years of peace in exchange for a few day's toil. It was time to focus. Where could he go? When? There had to be a time, a civilisation so advanced that problems like his were mere trifles. A race of new Romans or Atlanteans, or genetic super-beings, or something. Some kind and benevolent race, that was important, that was superior, and on Earth this time. No alien dimensions or weird places.

"Computer. Find the most advanced benevolent civilisation in Earth's entire history."

The little red lights blinked. A regular tip-tapping tapped and tipped. A few seconds passed. On the opposite wall the red digits of the electronic clock blinked from 22:51 to 22:52.

"Located," said the cold voice.

"Open gateway," said George.

Chapter Seven

The scene beyond the ring was a thick green jungle, unpleasantly warm, and unpleasantly humid. A curious sickly smell drifted towards him, something like rotting fruit with a smattering of decay, a scent of hope with a soupçon of death. The fragments of sky were salmon-pink.

George stepped through onto a sodden floor, noting the unsuitability of his patent leather footwear. A huge dragonfly landed on the back of his hand and waved its wings in greeting. It helicoptered away and George followed it, arcing his vision, and breathing in the hot vaporous atmosphere like an aquanaut in an exotic tepid bath. He was definitely in some sort of tropical rainforest. The trees were uncommonly tall, their rough bark stabbed with irregular thorns like a vicious pineapple, stretching upwards, towards wide sweeping palms of shattered black glass. The leaves near him were coated in a thick wax, and a syrupy moisture dripped from them, echoing the sweat he had already accumulated. There were no birds.

He crunched forwards, pressing aside the wide leaves and taking a frustratingly long time to peel away lines of tendril that stuck to his clothing like annoying magnets.

Where were the people? What was this civilisation? Why had the portal opened in the middle of nowhere? He had to trust it, and had to explore. The place, for all its unusualness, its remoteness, seemed safe enough, assuming that there were no diseases. He winced at the thought as he accidentally pressed a palm into the sticky mess on the outside of a tree. It smelled of rotten honey. He wiped the residue on his trousers and rubbed his hands in a forlorn attempt to clean off the rest. Everywhere looked the same, trees and green thickness. It was dark and oppressive, and he moved slowly, eager to keep in mind, if not in sight, the exact location of the portal, in case he had to leave. He shuddered at the thought of creepy things entering his laboratory, his house. What was this place?

He pushed on, keen to flatten a path. There was hiss and a crack ahead, the first sign of a living thing. He froze and listened, peering intently through the finger-fronds of thinning vegetation. He made a few tentative toe-steps, creeping behind a plant that looked like ivy but with huge plate leaves that were taller than George himself. Peeling back a leathery leaf he laid his first eyes on the creature.

Beyond was an oval clearing, edged with vast leaves with golden stalks, rather like rhubarb. Munching one of the leaves was a four legged dinosaur. It was the size of a cow, a big cow. It had thick scaly skin; khaki and green, with chitinous spikes, like huge rose thorns, of a light-brown hue, matching the colour and design of the spiked trees' bark. It was facing away, innocuously grazing. George held his breath and observed the fascinating creature.

The noise of breaking branches, some way in the distance, alerted them both. The creature raised its head and twisted it to the side, frozen, detecting every molecule of scent and every fragment of sound. George decided to step backwards, grasping for the smooth trunk of a bamboo-like plant. The startled creature instantly heard and then saw him, then gulped down a cheekful of bitter, crispy salad. George froze. Most creatures, he thought, responded to movement. At this point George really hoped that the creature hadn't seen him, even though it was obvious that it had. Perhaps closing his eyes would help? Perhaps, even if he were to be attacked and die right now, closing his eyes would help?

George didn't close his eyes. In fact, the most amazing thing happened. The creature turned towards him and said, in a rather plummy voice: "Ooh? Hello. I'm afraid I've no time to converse. I'm going to be killed by a tyrannosaurus rex in six seconds." George stood agape. He was about to say something, to at least stutter a vowel, when an enormous explosion of tree fragments kicked his legs from under him, and plopped him straight down on the floor with a painful bump. A gigantic two-legged lizard had leapt into the clearing, and in an instant, had grabbed the neck of the cow-creature, and begun to crush it in its vast pincer jaws with the most awful crunching sound. George pushed his body into the peaty soil, kicking and swimming backwards, desperate for cover. He squeezed past a log and sat motionless, peering at the scene through arcs of quivering fern.

A short distance away stood the biggest most terrifying monster he had ever seen. It was a huge brown lizard about as tall as a house, standing on two bulbous legs, and with twisty little arms. To George it looked like a *Tyrannosaurus rex*, and it undoubtedly was. It wrenched its great neck violently to the side and ripped the head off the lizard-cow, tossing it a vast distance away through webs of startled branches. Hot blood gushed from the open neck. The jungle stank like an abattoir. George gulped, and remained motionless, careful not to make a single sound and desperate not to waft even the faintest hint of a smell.

The bloody monster exhaled, spraying the clearing with a mist of saliva. There was a booming crackle and a second, larger tyrannosaur stepped in nonchalantly. It spoke in the sort of voice that an upper-middle class cave with a sore throat might have: "Well done. Good clean kill."

His friend responded: "I decided to go straight below the occipital condyle, severing at the atlas premaxilla construct that is most fascinating in this species."

"He wouldn't have felt a thing. You'll do well when I'm gone."

"How long have you got again?"

"Most probably three weeks. I'm going to be savaged in the ribs by a thrashing triceratops, and then die soon after him of hypovolemic shock."

"I've got years yet, impossible to say. Let's not dwell," said the smaller beast.

"Indeed," said the larger monster, in a surprisingly cheery tone for something the size of a double decker bus that had just discussed its violent demise, then: "Goodbye to you, old chap," while tapping a toe on the back of the deceased. He continued: "Come on, we don't want to be late. I do believe it's... this way."

At that point, the large one nodded to the sky and wheeled away, stepping over the end of the hulking corpse and stomping through the erect trees on the opposite end of the clearing, bashing a tunnel through the forest with a thundering crish, crunch, smish, smash. His smaller friend followed, wafting his great head side to side with a bouncy nod. George sat there, stunned, for a few silent moments. The last dregs of blood slopped from the corpse, making a sound like the last gulps of water leaving a summer bath drainpipe.

The tail twitched, one last enquiry to the absent brain. A last forlorn: "Hello?"

George let out a long breath, and sat wide eyed. Dinosaurs?! Dinosaurs that spoke English?!! How could these be the guardians of the greatest civilisation in history? Wait though... could his machine have played a trick? Perhaps this was the distant future instead... where dinosaurs had re-evolved... no. No! That's hardly likely. Everything about this place looked pre-historic. This must be the right place. The right time. If dinosaurs could speak then perhaps they could have a civilisation. Did they have a technology? Based on what he knew about fossils there couldn't have been one, not so much as a stick. Is technology necessary for civilisation?

George was distracted by a movement. A tiny mouse or shrew with light brown fur was sitting at George's feet. It had stopped, shivering and looking nervous while it sniffed the air. "Hello," said George, in his friendliest, most diplomatic voice. "How do you do?" The mouse paid no attention. It blinked and hurried on about its business, vanishing into a distant bush. "I suppose my ancestors weren't so smart after all," George quipped.

He stood up and brushed off his trousers. The soil was rich and dry, flaky, with a potato sort of smell that was not unpleasant.

Now what? He had to trust his computer. If this was a civilisation then there must be at least diplomats, and if they speak his language, so much the better. He moved into the clearing and took a curious look at the dead beast. Prostrate it was a little taller than George, and had a row of huge yellow spikes along its back like emerging teeth. He touched its scaly skin and found it warm. It had the texture of crisped cellophane. He slapped it, sending a ripple across the fatty dome.

"Goodbye to you, old chap," he said quietly.

There was a noise behind him and a whoosh of air. He wheeled around to find himself nose to nose with a gently smiling dinosaur. This one was like the tyrannosaurs but smaller, about George's height, some sort of raptor. One of its enquiring eyebrows was raised above keen eyes that stared at George like a cat observing a mouse.

George froze in wide-eyed terror. Every corpuscle squeezed some life from his hands and face and feet and gave it generously to his heart and brain. The raptor didn't react, then blinked like a lazy student with a hangover. Wheels in George's brain began to turn. After a short pause which seemed to be very long indeed, he stammered a phrase while desperately trying not to appear like a wimp: "H-hello. I come in peace..!"

The raptor blinked again and sank back, pursed its lips, and let out a long "Hmm..." and then: "I don't expect you know where this thing is?", in a tone that seemed rhetorical.

"Um, what?"

"The conference," intoned the beast, "It's around here somewhere." He waved a head back and forth a few times in rapid reptilian jumps, searching for clues.

George began to relax. His blood began to stroll back to its rightful place like children going back inside school after a fire drill. He looked carefully at this remarkable creature. The flesh around the golden eyes was iridescent blue and as beautiful as the most delicate butterfly. The eyebrows were red and coarse, like feathers protruding from scales that seemed to consist of banks of short hard hair. There was certainly a spark of something brilliant behind his glassy irises. Most importantly he seemed friendly, actually rather likeable.

"My name is George. I've come a long way to visit here, across time and space. I'm a scientist..."

The creature was now peering over George's shoulder at the

corpse. He raised his eyebrows in surprise.

"Goodness gracious!" He gave a hop past George and looked up and down the body. "Tyrannosaurus rex, no doubt. Neat job." He licked some of the fresh blood, then twisted his head back to look at George. "My name is Philodor Karakticus, astroheliologist. I assume you're coming to the conference? We should leave now or we will be sixteen seconds late."

Philodor leaned back and stretched his tense shoulders like a cat in the morning sun. He looked down the tunnel in the trees that the pair of tyrannosaurs had taken, then flitted out a thin red tongue to taste the air, casting a single keen eye at George, waiting. George wiped his hands and moved towards the shimmering dinosaur, picking his way over the fragmented terrain like a cautious heron. Philodor then strode off like an ostrich, lifting bunches of his toes in a smooth cycle, before pressing them down, spread wide, into the soft floor. George had to jog to keep up.

"What is the conference about?" enquired George between jogs.

"I thought you'd ask that. Well, you see, it's all very exciting! I've calculated that the sun is going to explode. I think I'm the first person to think of it."

George was somewhat taken aback by this and paused jogging. He decided not to harm his relationship with this creature by arguing about whether and how the sun was or wasn't going to explode. He ran some small steps to catch up. "Wait a minute. You said think of it? Did you use a computer?"

"Computers? Oh, we don't need machines. I mean mental arithmetic." He stopped walking. "I know what you're going to ask me next."

"Do you?"

"Yes. You're going to ask me what three hundred and fifty six thousand, two hundred and forty seven, multiplied by two million, seven hundred and eighty one thousand, three hundred and seven was, and the answer is nine hundred and ninety billion, eight hundred and thirty two million, two hundred and seventy four thousand, eight hundred." And with that he strode onwards again, at speed. George ran to catch up.

"What made you think I was going to ask you that?!" asked an astonished George (who, as it turns out, probably was).

Philodor paused again and looked and George with a raised eyebrow. "You have a very large brain."

George smiled proudly. "Oh, well..."

"You wouldn't understand," said Philodor, again moving off. "Our ancestor's brains got smaller and smaller, our thoughts faster and faster. My brain is many factors of ten more powerful than yours. My race can calculate every possibility and see every probable future to such a fine degree that we can calculate every event for months or years in advance. It's trifling for us to predict the lumbering thought patterns of big brained fauna such as yourself. I can practically see the wheels in your head turning."

George should have been quite insulted, but instead felt awed. There was something about the quality of intelligence that was instantly detectable. Just as it was easy to see a cat lazily eyeing a yapping dog with an inherent sense of superiority, it was also easy to see a squirrel eyeing a cat in the same way, and next to Philodor, George was that yapping dog, rolling around, tongue out on the wet lawn, jumping cross-eyed in circles at its flailing tail, while Philodor was sat by the grass, leg over leg, discussing philosophy and playing chess with the tyrannosaurs.

But the dinosaurs didn't write philosophy. They didn't write anything! Not so much as a scrawled note to a cave-milkman. Or invent anything for that matter. Or do anything, or show any signs of intelligence whatsoever!

"You're about to ask me why we didn't invent anything." presumed Philodor. George raised a forehead of submission to this before saying: "Yes."

"The answer is simple. We can work out all of the answers in an instant, and so don't need a machine to help, and we don't need to tell anyone because they can work out the answers too. In fact, we can predict the question before its asked and see, almost instantly, every possible answer."

George paused to absorb this information, then whipped out a question. "But there's more to technology than machines to calculate. What about factories, farms, things to make life more comfortable? Where are the buildings, the palaces, the luxuries of civilisation?"

"I thought you were going to ask that. It's difficult to convey how we think. I'm not sure if your simian neurology is capable of imagining infinite knowledge. Look, here." The dinosaur stopped in his tracks. He bent his head to the right and waved a gracious claw down. There was an ants nest on the floor, a rectangular structure made of mud, like a pyramid. A trail of large black ants were carrying leaf segments, while other ants stood guard at the boundaries.

"Observe the shape of this nest," continued Philodor. "What if it was made more angular, or larger, or from marble, or from steel, with internal heating, powered by batteries, or powered by the sun, or geothermally, with robot ants, to guard, to fetch food, slaves, with machines to care for the baby ants, or create baby ants, or what if baby ants could be grown in tubes, or made as robots with baby ant brains so that they never deteriorated with age or suffered the pains of life. What if the ants were bigger, better to defend themselves from predators, better to mould the world to their whim, to use its resources, cut down trees, invent new types of tree, or use metal trees from new alloys that lasted forever, and train other species to perform jobs for them, made other species, or used genetically targeted viruses to transform creatures into better ones, and eliminate the creatures they disliked."

Philodor paused. George said nothing.

"I could continue forever drawing that tree of possibility. Now, see the whole tree from afar. When you can see every possibility, each is equally pointless. No one path is better than any other, they are just different. To an ant, a fragment of a leaf is joy embodied, just as you enjoy your simian pleasures. We can see every possible pleasure and so experience none."

There was a sudden glance of sadness in Philodor's eyes as he looked along the path towards the distant conference. "No one life is better than any other, so we live simply, as nature intended."

He moved off, away from the busy ants. George followed, in silent thought, listening to the crish crunch of their steps. If you knew everything then knowledge would be pointless, and if you could see every possibility, could see the truth of your own insignificance, and even the time and circumstances of your own death, then your life would be pointless.

Philodor was a distance away now, racing ahead and leaving George ambling behind. They had been climbing uphill almost constantly. The dense arcs of fern had gradually fallen away, and a clear path had widened into an avenue of tall, thin trees topped with fists of black needles. Up ahead was a wide, but rugged, field made of lumps of stone, tiny clover-like plants, and wet yellow-green moss. It was like a wild Scottish moor, but the air was warm. The trees fell away completely. A bird screamed by, a flying reptile, and George was left standing in the open in bright sunshine. They had arrived.

The space was a high domed hilltop, surrounded on three sides by the crescent jungle like arms hugging the hill. The open side had a breathtaking view over miles of sunlit yellow-green landscape, broken by intermittent flecks of unusual trees and the occasional rocky outcrop. The place was humming with dinosaurs of all sizes, from giant plant eating behemoths with great muscular necks, to brilliantly coloured beasts the size of horses, with iridescent green fleshy frills and golden needle spines. The flying thing swirled, screamed again, and landed to join a cluster of white ribbed bird-like reptiles with very long faces, jabbering and shaking like giggling old ladies. In the middle was a cube of stone, a natural altar made of coarse rock that looked like it had fallen there, with a plop, from outer space.

A silky, crimson creature slinked onto the cube and roared to the sky, puffing out a rippling mane of many colours around his wide neck. He looked somewhat like a cat, as large as two tigers, with powerful shoulders and wide padded paws, all covered in thick, soft fur of cherry red. Everyone stopped chattering and settled down. George sat down on the soft mossy top, propping himself up. He was tired now and his head, so well behaved in the jungle, was now glowing and feeling strange. He wondered if the dense patch inside it, that chaotic nodule growing out of control was thinking, making him think like the dinosaurs.

"Welcome!" roared the leader. "Welcome all. Accelerator One is now complete and with it our civilisation has reached the paragon of possibility!"

The crowd erupted into rapturous cheers and squawks. George wondered what Accelerator One was.

"Worse news!" spoke the leader majestically. The crowd again hushed. "Worse news, comes from our helioscientists. I'll let Professor Philodor Karakticus explain."

Philodor swayed towards the altar. He stepped up and addressed the crowd with a high head. "As many of you know, our sun is a self-sustained nuclear reaction that is broadly stable, with intermittent periods of chaotic instability. Recent calculations suggest that its power is increasing and within five billion years will engulf the Earth!" There were gasps from the crowd. "Worse still, in considerably less than one billion years the surface temperature of the planet will be sufficiently hot to heat the oceans and cause a runaway temperature increase that would inevitably end all life!"

There was a silent pause. After a few seconds a voice shouted: "He's right, I've just performed the calculation." Then another voice said, "Yes. It's true." The crowd began to chatter and hum at this news.

George wasn't impressed. Of course, he knew the sun wouldn't last forever, or the Earth. It wasn't news that in billions of years the planet might be in trouble.

"We have to decide now!" boomed the authoritarian voice of the leader. His tail swished into the air, drawing curls in the evening sky with its white tip. "Shall we deploy Accelerator One?"

There was that phrase again, although this time he used the worrying word "deploy". Was this a weapon, something dangerous? An army... but called One? Was there an Accelerator Two? He did say this one was just finished. Oh, too much thinking! George's tired brain was rifling through options like a Philodor. He closed his eyes and lay down. The floor was wonderfully soft and warm, like a Sunday morning bed. He must remember to ask Philodor if he knows of a cure for his aching brain. He must remember to ask. The debate continued as he rested.

"We are arguing for two futures, one of ignorance and simple pleasures, and one of infinite power yet emotional sterility. This is a unique juncture. Every choice we envisage will produce the same result, except the choice to smash the choices. To plunge ourselves and our possibilities into darkness. We, as a race, have the chance to reset."

George was lost in his own thoughts like a monkey in parliament fascinated only by the colour of a particularly striking apple. He propped himself up again and noticed lots of tiny black flies swimming around in the cooling air. The sun was setting, and the sky above was streaked with the most beautiful orange clouds, peppering the dark blue backdrop of this pollution-free planet. He was beginning to feel hungry and his mind ran back through the trees, to the portal, his basement, and his family. How lovely a roast beef dinner would be right now, or some chicken and rice and peas, opposite his wife, sipping a crisp white wine. That was his first proper meal with Pauline, back when they first met. They had been seeing each other for a few weeks and the warmth of love was in them both. How special that meal was, would always be, to George at least. How sad it would be to leave her. "At least," thought George, "we're not in love any more." A tiny fly buzzed its wings, and lifted off from George's arm to join the cluster of his friends flying above.

The dinosaurs exploded into hoots and cheers, pulling George from his dream. Something had just happened. What had he missed? Oh why couldn't he pay attention!? The seated dinosaurs stood up and some of the winged creatures took to the skies. On the central rock, the magnificent leader nodded with happy pride: "Then let it be done."

George became worried and quickly rose to his feet. Philodor was in sight, his iridescent head bobbing between the necks and horns of other fantastic beasts. George tried to catch his eye. What had they all agreed to? It sounded dangerous. He needed to know what was happening. Philodor noticed George and pushed through the crowd towards him.

"What's happened? What is Accelerator One?" George hurriedly asked. He could tell that Philodor was about to say something along the lines of: "I thought you were going to say that," but he restrained himself and skipped that part of the conversation.

"It's a weapon designed to end all life on Earth. It's a vast, clastic, igneous formation with spherical eutaxitic bands." He paused, observing the blank look on George's face. "It's a giant rock that uses a volcano to fire it into space. It will orbit around for a year or two and then crash into the Earth, killing everything. Well, nearly everything."

George suddenly realised the truth. The dinosaurs had just voted for their own extinction. He gulped, and a lump of gooey discomfort squished up from his throat to an upper quadrant of his head. He remembered why he came.

Philodor was looking at the fantastic streams of sunset clouds, quite distant.

"Philodor..." George interrupted, "I'm dying. I've got a brain tumour."

"I'm not surprised, given the size of the thing," joked the raptor. He saw that George wasn't in the mood for jokes. George continued: "Have you got anyone here who can help me? That's why I'm here. That's why I came. Can you can help?"

Philodor smiled gently. "Don't worry about that my dear little simian friend. We'll all be dead in ninety four seconds..."

He was cut short. The ground had started to rumble, then all of a sudden it shifted violently to the side, knocking George to the ground with a bump. A long, deep, boom like distant thunder hummed through everyone's body. The dinosaurs began to scatter, some darting away, some moving more slowly, the strong wide necks of the truly gigantic plant eaters undulating left and right like rubber palm trees. There was a hiss, and an explosion of steam erupted from a patch of ground in the distance, throwing a clod of earth the size of a car into the sky. Philodor had turned to look towards the megalithic altar. The leader was sitting majestically on top, smiling with the contentment of a Siamese cat that thought it owned the planet. This cat probably did.

The floor heaved upwards, rolling George flat on his back. He clambered to his feet in a rush, sliding the soles of his shoes on the moss causing it to leap off and cascade in rubbery bumps over the stone floor. The type of stone looked the same as the altar in the centre. This whole hilltop was one giant lump of rock. The realisation hit George: this whole hilltop was one giant lump of rock that was about to be blown fifty miles straight up, into outer space, around the sun twice, then down again with a smash!

It was time to go. George turned, and assumed the stature of a sprinter on the starting blocks as he faced the jungle he had emerged from. The royal-blue sky was drowning into an inky blackness, and the way ahead was deep and dark and obscure. He thought he knew the way he came, but he had no time to think. With a mighty boom another blast of steam rocketed skywards. It was the starting pistol that set him running. Leg over leg, foot over moss over bracken, fern, crusted leaf, soil, mud, twig, slime. This was the right way, down the avenue of tall trees that were now giving a fresh pine scent. The ground hiccuped violently, and a shower of needles from the trees rained with a hissing sound onto the thick green canopy. George slowed down, panting, lungs burning. His head was pulsating pain in time with his rapid heartbeat. Must get home. He marched forwards as fast as he could manage, pushing through the soft mud, and now the tight ferns that had first greeted him that morning. It was dark now, very dark. Somewhere here was a huge dinosaur corpse that would guide him, but where? The path trodden by those giant tyrannosaurs was obvious in the day but now he couldn't see a thing.

The floor began to vibrate now, not wide and violently like before, but gently, like a helicopter warming up the engine. This was more worrying. At any moment everything could explode. Explode and kill him, here, in the ancient past, now, and miles from anywhere and anyone while he was searching for salvation. Oh the irony!

"Maybe I could climb a tree..." he thought but the idea was ludicrous. There were no branches on these spined poles. Keep looking. Keep moving. That's the best plan. Somewhere here is a clearing and a giant dead body...

Then he saw it: a light, up ahead, glinting like a distant star, a lighthouse casting a steady, but tiny, beam. Of course, that was it, his portal. The gate was open and his basement lights were on. Oh thank God for electricity! In daylight he might not even have seen it. He eagerly stomped his way forwards, rubbing, tearing through the defensive vegetation that clawed at his legs and clothes like a pleading ex-lover. Tighter and tighter the tendrils gripped as he pushed harder and harder towards the nearing portal, ripping through the dense luscious vines like an avid weeder, his limbs pulled back by the strings as though George were a puppet controlled by the master of nature, and all of the time, the constant shake of the ground, the forest, the sky, and world, attacked him.

But now here it was, the gateway, and safety, and home. The ground gave a mighty belch and pushed George through the portal. He landed face down on the hard floor in his basement, his clothes shredded and spattered with dirt. He was dragging a polite trail of green tendrils that gripped him all over with micro-spines. He was exhausted.

He blinked slowly and blew heavy breaths over the smooth floor. His eyes focused on a tiny beetle a few centimetres from his face. It was a ladybird with violet-silver wings, and was happily exploring the laboratory with the wonder of a small child. Its rounded shell clicked open and the visitor whirred upwards, beyond the range of George's tired eyes.

"Close gateway," George uttered.

Chapter Eight

George lay on the cool floor until his rapid breathing had slowed to a regular, calm pace. He peeled himself up, and slumped into the soft leather puffs of his office chair, his arms loosely drooping floorwards. A deep and welcome feeling of peace flowed through him. He felt tired but not unwell. His head felt fine, and his thoughts and memory were as acute as every thought and memory had been before. The glowing numbers of the clock opposite flashed a new minute. Time was short, just the same. A shiver of fear ran through him and pulled him back to consciousness. Why did he run from death in the dinosaur's realm when he was going to die soon anyway? It was a natural response. A panic reaction.

"I wonder..." he whispered to himself.

Could there be an afterlife that he could visit? He had tried heaven, perhaps then a hell... just a glimpse, to appease his worries. He didn't have to go, just look. The idea became interesting. Hell - every culture had one. Of course! Why didn't he think of it before? He could see what only saints and visionaries had, and all safely.

"Computer," he commanded: "Find hell."

Initially nothing seemed to happen. The red dots of the computer continued their jazzy moves as if no command had been given. Then, one of the florescent lights in the ceiling began to buzz, then flicker, like the wings of a trapped moth. An ear close to the smooth warm glass would hear a tapping, a rapping, a quiet atomic and subatomic march, the start of a wave, growing and growing. Invisible, and as yet undetectable by the large and clumsy senses of the man below.

George took a step forwards, and as he clamped his foot down, the room instantly became dark and silent. The normally ever-present hum of the air purification units and computer fans in his laboratory was now gone. There was no sound at all; even his exhale was silent. He spoke, well, he tried to speak, and to shout, but there was nothing - and yet he could hear his heart, the pulsing fluid rush of blood swishing and sploshing in regular thrusts: squish squash squish squash.

A crackle of white-noise appeared, somewhere. He held out his hand and noticed that, despite the blackness of his surroundings, he could see it. The flesh was faint grey, lit seemingly from every angle, as though he were inside an electron microscope or an x-ray machine. He looked up, and could now perceive the room too. It was also grey, just visible, faint outlines that traced and caressed every hard edge, running in lines like threads of potential tactility. These lines grew brighter, and in a short time he noticed particles in the air, floating, like soft snowflakes on the pinkest of Christmas evenings, waltzing gently in the mystical omni-light. The flakes were moving, pulled by some as yet unfeelable force towards the gateway. Gradually, more particles began to form, and more sucked into the hollow ring, forming a shape, visible in blue-grey, the walls of a tunnel, growing brighter and brighter, more vivid as more particles appeared in the room, and were pulled into the long tube beyond the gate. The rough walls of the tunnel were rotating slowly, a smooth tumble like the inside of a great machine. In the distance there was a tiny white light which glittered like an unreachable star. George crept towards the ring and leaned inside, hesitant to step through. There didn't appear to be an actual floor.

"Now what?" he thought.

The light in the distance was mesmerisingly beautiful. It seemed to be drawing him in, moving closer and closer, as though he were flying towards it. Without realising how, George found himself inside the tunnel, floating in the air, upright like a swimmer treading water. He noticed though that he was moving backwards, not forwards. He felt uncomfortable, but tried to relax into the sensation, holding on to any fragments of its pleasure. It can be just as nice to move backwards as forwards, he reasoned. But part of him knew he was lying to himself, and a spark of unease began to grow into a fear, and as the feeling grew he began to slide backwards more quickly, and as his speed grew his fear grew, wheel upon wheel, in an unstoppable cycle. The tunnel walls began to slip away, then fly away, faster and faster, the tiny white star more distant, colder, receding and shrinking; hope being choked, ungraspable, going, going, faster and faster, the fear growing to terror, down and down, away from light towards darkness, backwards, in ultimate horror and then, suddenly, jerked violently downwards, down a shaft and cast into a pit, one pit in a sea of pits, like a pepperpot world. He was at the bottom of a black muddy well in an infinite plain of holes.

A faint, cold starlight filtered in from some unseen place above. George was cowering, afraid, in a heap on the gritty floor. "Please!" he whimpered. "Please get me out!" His skin burned and prickled with feverish anxiety. "Computer..." cried his weak voice, already devoid of hope.

"There are no computers here," whispered a clear voice near to his ear. The voice had no location, no space or width. George shakily raised his head. A curl of grey mist twisted like a matador's cape, and pulled into the shape of a devil with taut red skin. His gargoyle face was triangular, sporting a short, pointed black beard, and topped with two neat horns. Slitted yellow eyes shone with a curious waltz of fear and amusement. He had dark, animal legs covered in thin hair, cloven hooves, and was naked, sporting a large erect penis, wet and shiny, that nodded with his pulse.

"You'll never escape!" said the voice, mirroring George's caged panic, and knowledge, the terrible truth. Why was he so stupid!? Why did he want to visit hell of all places? He closed his eyes and felt the ring of pain in his head, a ring like a iron doughnut-bell vibrating an ache around the inside of his body. Shutting out the vision only intensified his feelings. His eyes opened to face the devil, vivid and terrifying. He could see each tiny detail, each fold of skin, each hair, dancing and swaying like smoke with each motion, but also locked, rigid, explicit, sharp - and every fragment of the demon's features shone fear.

George dug in with his feet and pushed back into the black gritty soil, slopping his hand into a pool of foul smelling liquid. He glanced down and saw the devil's reflection in a puddle. The demon seemed to recoil, as if frightened himself. An unexpected shock of pleasure shot through George at the sight, a yellow shock, that raced from the middle of his back and up his electric skin to the base of his head. He pushed into the mud, jolting backwards in panic on his stalk limbs like a drunken spider. His back hit the hard wall with a thud, and still unblinking, he looked up at the face of the devil. George's fear gripped him more tightly, and the angular face of the beast became more vivid. His slit eyes widened in a pleasure taken from George's discomfort. The beast rolled his head back, and the space around him began to move, change, distort as though alive with barely perceptible tentacles, dark forms that danced an obscene, writhing dance of ecstasy.

"Yesssss....." hissed the devil as he closed his eyes, rolling a smile back, up and round. The creature flexed a heavy claw and his stiff penis, chasing each gram of pleasure. Finding and biting and eating each sparkling fragment of some delight.

A sudden recognition leapt into George's mind. He had seen this creature before, when he was a child, afraid, cowering under his bed covers. That unseen thing, the thing in his room that he feared had a form, a shape, an idea, and it looked like this demon. The demon was there, hiding in the unseen corners. This face was built from fragments of shadows and folds in cloth. It was there, watching the frightened child with a keen enjoyment.

An image of war jumped into George's mind, a modern battlefield and a young, dying soldier. In the corner of the scene, unglanced by the concerned bystanders, hid the demon, a twisting grey shape in the malformed landscape. It was staring at the frightened soldier. Smiling but malevolent. Sucking pleasure from the terror in the eyes of the man. The soldier's bony hand tightly gripped and twisted a clod of soil, and as the grip became tighter the face in the corner became more vivid, the features stronger. The eyes lit more brightly with delight. The soldier's hand relaxed, limp, dead, and the demon faded into smoke, a smoke that curled and flowed, like a matador's cape, into blackness.

There was a white flash and George was in the pit once more. He was alone and felt calmer now. The space felt large, wide, like the base of a tall chimney that grew and grew upwards for a great distance to touch a faint blue circle of sky, or something like it, high above. A smooth disc, like an unreachable dinner plate. Distant hope. As small as a pea at arms length.

He stared at the moon-like shape. It remained still, immobile, unchanging. The eye of a distant mother, staring at a child through a telescope, a long bent tube of mottled stone that snaked backwards towards a memory of home, a laboratory, a family and friendship. Somewhere along that conduit was a wife and a son. Perhaps outside, perhaps busy with mundane earthly tasks, thinking with occasional, curious lightning-strokes about George and his eternal frantic work; work on his machine, that thing that he loves more than them.

Every segment of this situation was born from every cell of George. There was no input from others. No collaboration was needed on his machine, and there was probably nobody on the entire planet who could have helped him build it anyway. It was somehow fitting that George should make a transportation machine single handed and use it to take himself, and nobody else, to a unique isolated place in the universe. This hell might as well be his own creation. These gritty walls might be the texture of his own arteries up close. Yes! Perhaps this place was that very thing. Perhaps each speck of mud was a fragment of some cellular decay, the vomited ruins of a moribund blood-cell or lump of black dust once sucked in on a lazy Sunday-bed morning and forever trapped in a fold of a lung like a dark and absurd award trophy, an award for simply living. Here is your machine; your great device to change the world and fix humanity, repair its flaws. Cure its diseases. A machine for everybody, and yet used by nobody. Used only by George. Known only to George. Tested by him to repair him and take him to; where? His own self? A hell of an empty home. What is the point of a cure when to survive would mean nothing to anyone? When existence benefits nobody but the sole survivor? To live or to die would be equally pointless to the only creature in the universe. Life and death would be the same.

And here, in this universe, there was nobody. Here in this pit in a sea of pits. In a sea of seas. All holes, holes awaiting prisoners. Waiting, ever waiting for the touch of a human hand or mind, an occupier to give meaning to the jail. A sentence of a year to a solitary prisoner is a sentence of eternity minus one year to the prison, the hollow shell. An empty home is not a home.

George looked again at the unchanging disc. Around its rim there were no stars. No silver dust of awe and beauty. No sign, no hope of other eyes looking back. No hope of other distant minds thinking about the distant man lost in the pit. There was nothing but blackness. The black edges of a black tunnel of immeasurable length. There was no sound either, no wind or hums or chatter, just the smooth flow of thought through the loose wet channels of a young mind. Time was treading water, in stasis. Hovering like a bow drawn and creeping over a single cello string. Like a hand over a flat lake, touching the magic, electric air that lives in the tiny space over the surface of cold, glass water.

This was the essence of existence, a liquid nothingness coalesced into a droplet of emptiness. George's work had ended, at home and out of reach forever. Somewhere back there his papers were sitting. Some neatly arranged, some haphazardly left with half a sentence, part of an equation scrawled out. A note of a melody, waiting to be finished. A shopping list, uncollected. Bills paid and unpaid. Boxes of old rubbish, too precious to throw away, just in case they might be useful one day. Now, soon, they will be picked up by young relatives and unpacked. Curiously filed through. Those yellow thin sheets, school reports. Old letters that mean nothing to anyone except George. Precious things that lose their value upon death, their soul instantly vanished. The papers will be measured and discarded. Given away and thrown away. The bills paid then recycled. The furniture sold off to young couples who ignore the dents, marks, scratches that were born from knocks made by the giant sand-grains that tumbled from the great hour-glass of a life. The basement will be cleaned, and swept and hoovered. The wide snakes of coils of wire will be curled and wrapped into neat hoops and sold. The machine's great rings scrapped and buried outside under tangles of steel hair and rusty bedsprings, and the empty wooden basement, like a hollow Spanish galleon, will be glanced at one last time before the light is clicked off, and the room will be left, and the house sold, and each memory exhaled with it.

And then, we come here. A place where time was dead. A breathless ocean. The air itself seemed stationary, as though each exhale was secretly and instantly replaced with an inhale elsewhere. The light was dark grey, everywhere. Dark grey and cold, like the light from a newly extinguished candle that chases the last ray of heat, the last red run from the smoking wick, an expanding orb of coldness like a black-hole mushroom, the ghost of what was once light and heat. This pit was a void. The walls, the pool, everything, the detritus of its own slow decay. Ruts on a sandstone slab, cut by season after season of cold rain. Bit away by green lichen teeth, crunching and etching away the written details: a name. A date. Cause of death. An unreadable blur. Grey, black, gritty. A forgotten melted lump.

George noticed that he was looking at himself from above. He was floating in some indefinable part in the chimney and looking down at the huddled figure of his thinking self. The walls and floor, so keenly felt by his cold limbs, were as good as invisible from this perspective and the man seemed to be a speck in a sea of blackness. The darkness, the nothingness surrounding the man seemed to grow, become more solid and imposing. George could still hear his thoughts, his chatter about emptiness, fragments of memory and observation, the bitter liquid thoughts spawned by isolation. Then he saw it, to the right of the man, in the dance of hissing speckles before his straining eyes. There was a shape, a figure, a face. It was the devil, the creature was feeding off the man. Feeding off the introverted energy of his solitude. The devil turned and looked at George above with an evil smile.

There was a white flash and the scene changed. George was still flying somewhere in this chimney, looking down. He could see a naked man now, crouched in a grainy corner, rolled into a ball and not moving. The man was very thin, the ribs were showing and his taut yellow skin was pulled tightly over his knobbly shoulders. The man slowly raised his head and extended an arm, letting it flop weakly to the dirty ground. The arm was skeletal, the fingers splayed like matchsticks. The fingers twitched, and crunched closed, ploughing channels in the black floor. A heavenly smell flowed by like an invisible ribbon. A warm food smell, wholesome and delicious, freshly baked bread, roasted meat, sweet pastries; all of these together and more. The smell cycled around the tunnel walls, gripping the lumpy rocky sides and cascading down like a glittering waterfall of deliciousness. With a great effort, the man below lifted his head to look up. Sunken eyes stared from a face devoid of fat, eyes above bony lumps. His mouth opened, gasping at the air, grasping at the smell, the hope of food. A tear appeared on the anaemic rim of his blinkless eye. Its saltless liquid ran over his sallow face, then off and down to the black nothing beneath. Then, George saw it again. Near the man. The demon. Watching him. It had lit up more brightly when the tear appeared, like a flash. A huddled creature of white mist, crouching, hiding, grinning, feeding.

George became more afraid; feeling that he was being watched too. He turned, and found himself on the floor of the pit again, shuffling among the dirt. There was nobody here but he didn't feel alone. He felt something in the space with him. Something indefinable, a malevolent presence. Something, some body, was watching him from a dark corner. It was the demon. He knew it. He could feel it. His fear grew as he sensed the creature. It was behind him, and to his right, on the fringes of his senses. He froze, trying to remain calm. Now he knew where it was, he could remain in control. He mustn't look. He leaned back, slowly, with great discipline, pushing against the wall so it couldn't sneak up behind him. He wasn't looking, trying to bury his fear. Trying not to think of it, but the more he tried to ignore it the stronger his fear grew. Stronger with each passing second. He could feel the creature close, feel its breath on his neck. No, must ignore it! Must blot it out!

"You can't escape me..." whispered the cold voice, with an unseen smile.

George clamped his eyes shut. The ring of pain sounded in his head, cycling round and round and round. Shaking and quivering a tone that reflected around his skull. Growing and pulsing like a bell. Screaming louder and louder. Must bear it! No! No! His panic had grown too large. He could hold it back no longer. His eyes flew open!

A grating voice moaned with pleasure: "Aaah..." A red glow materialised into moving figures. The wide-eyed devil was arched backwards, his muscular right arm was bent and clasping the back of his neck. Semen was spurting from his nodding penis, spattering warm over the naked back of a child cowering on all fours, its shadowed face turned away. George was paralysed, locked in a terrified gaze. The scene became increasingly vivid, dull red became bright scarlet, glistening white highlights from wet skin pierced into George's retina like needles. The sickening smell of sexual fluids choked the test-tube crucible of the pit. The atmosphere thick, and hot, and humid. Choking. Not enough air. He tried to breath more, to suck some oxygen from the syrupy gasses he felt pass into his throat, carbon dioxide, carbon monoxide, heavy and unbreathable.

The child extended an arm, clamping down a scrawny, quivering hand from shadow into light, clawing the raspy floor with coarse yellow nails. George saw that the top of the arm was blistered with bulbous sores, red balloons of disease ready to pop their vile liquids in burning agony. From the pustules down, the skin was white with heaving infection, a rank blotch, edged with black and green rotted flesh. George felt dizzy, hot, his skin running like ants. It was too much. Too much! He clamped his eyes shut. Blackness. Blackness was his hope, his salvation. Nothingness. Shut out the world. "Make it go AWAY!"

Silence.

"If you think that's scary," said the voice, "you should try dying."

Chapter Nine

George opened his eyes wide, and pulled in a sharp breath. He was slumped in his leather office chair in his basement lab. He flashed some fervent looks around. The gateway was empty. The lights above were cool and steady. There was nobody here. He was safe. The quietness helped soothe his racing heart. He gradually calmed down then sat up with a soft cloth crunch. His clothes were torn and muddy from his dinosaur trip. Had he just been to hell? It didn't matter. A dream, a vision, a reality. The message was the same. He hoped not to see the devil again.

One thing was true, however, he felt hungry. It was time to pause his adventures and take a break. His head was spread with a dull, spidering ache, but nothing intolerable. He slid open a hissing steel drawer and popped out two paracetamol tablets, gulping them down with a winced sip of mineral water. He stood up and plodded towards the stairs, up and through the slatted white wooden door to the house above.

A helical pink stream of paper drifted past his face as he entered the evening hallway. There were brightly coloured balloons taped in the corners. Pauline hummed past him. "Good evening dear!" she said, giving him a peck on the cheek. She smelled nice.

"What's going on?" George enquired.

"Hoo hoo hoo! We're having a party for you!" smiled his wife, bouncing towards the living room. "Come on, everybody's here!"

George wheeled right, and followed his wife past the base of the stairs to enter a living room humming with smartly dressed people, some standing, some seated, balancing paper plates of salad and crispy bites beside tall glasses of fizzy yellow drinks, globes of dark wine and beer cans. The ceiling gripped arcs of streaming coloured ribbon. The television was on, just beside George, chattering and babbling something about planting. Ursula, Pauline's tiny mother, was plomped in a chair watching it and knitting, her face lit up by the fascinating flicker. She hadn't done any actual gardening in years.

"We thought you needed cheering up," beamed Pauline.

George slid towards the low rectangular table that was bedecked with plates of party nibbles. He grabbed a roast chicken wing and bit into its salty richness, then began to spoon coleslaw onto a plate, embellishing the meal with triangular sandwiches in white bread, smiles of peppered potato, and deliciously crisp and greasy sausage rolls.

Trevor from work touched his shoulder. "How are you doing

matey?"

"Hungry!" chomped George jokingly, then, "I'm okay. How about you?"

"Oh, I'm fine. Still upright. Things have gone a bit 'banana' since you left. I think you were the only one there who did any work. That Martin's a complete pranny. Are you coming back then? Come on! You know you want to." Trevor was always a good sort. Technically he was George's boss but they effectively shared the work fifty-fifty. It had been a few years now since the office days, the programming and dealing with clients, the regular money, the regular routine, and the banter. Leaving wasn't easy, but he needed the time to make Adam, and then work on his machine. Those things were more important to him.

"I'm okay." It's the best reply when asked how you are. It's not the answer that matters, it's that the question was there, because it implies concern. "Dying" would be a right downer. In this respect the French have achieved mastery with "Ça va?" which demands the same reply. I expect now that even they say "okay", like every country does, since World War Two. What a strange gift Hitler had indirectly given to everyone.

The two were interrupted by Pauline, who magically appeared

beside George: "You'll never guess who's here!" said her excited voice, then beamed, "Sorry, Trevor."

Trevor swallowed a nibble and nodded an acknowledgement.

"Is it... Leo Tolstoy?" quipped George.

"Now don't be silly," said Pauline. "It's David Prentiss. You know, the gardener from television."

George raised a brow of genuine surprise, and turned. A large, square man, with curly dark hair, smiled and shook his hand. It was a big, soft, boxing-glove of a hand with a gentle grip.

"Pleased to meet you, George. Your wife's been telling me about you." he said in warm vowels with a soupçon of Cornwall. "I'm sorry to hear about your illness. How do you feel about it?"

Feel about it? As opposed to how do you feel? George felt at ease.

"It's hard..." he began. "Defiant. Sad. It's difficult, you know. I don't know what to think."

David nodded and listened attentively, allowing George to speak in his own time. "I've, we've... known for some time. I'd been prepared for the worst, but it was still a shock."

Pauline spoke up with mad enthusiasm: "The flowers think everything will be just fine!"

David flashed a polite smile at this orange remark in the beige chat. "Well, we must always listen to the flowers. Pauline tells me that you're looking for a cure?"

"Yes," continued George. "In a way... I'm searching for one..."

David nodded gently. "I lost my wife, you know, not long after we were married. It took a long time, a lot of work before I came to terms with it. It was an accident... how she died, just a freak accident... she drowned. In a way that made it harder. I retreated into myself but eventually came though, thanks to my gardening. Joining a local group really helped me."

"Working alone here, I do miss getting out among people. I mean, half of the people here, I haven't seen them in years."

"Maybe you could join my group? Are you interested in gardening? We've got a few spaces if you'd like you join us?"

"No, sorry," said George "That's more my wife's area."

Besides, gardening is rather a long term task. It's an activity more like guiding a river than building a house, or a machine.

Perhaps the act of gardening is the important thing, not the garden. Thinking that it's too late to start something is a deadly trap for anyone, especially George.

"It's never too late," continued David. "Here, I've got you something..."

The gardener twisted a smile and from his pocket unfurled a small rectangular paper packet. He passed it to George.

"Sunflower seeds," he continued, "I knew Pauline liked them. Maybe you could plant one one day..?"

George looked the envelope over, reading the tiny writing. Pauline was overjoyed at this special gift and gave a solitary clap of glee. "Oooh - Mottley James! I've wanted these for ages. Oh, you're such a poppet, David."

She gave the gardener and hug and a peck, then hooked a loose but happy arm around George. David grinned awkwardly. "It's nothing, you enjoy them."

George thanked David and slid the seeds into his pocket. He stepped towards the glass-topped table and poured a goblet of white wine before sucking an acidic sip. It felt divine. Better than a warm, dry cotton towel on a cold damp day. Better than champagne in heaven. He closed his eyes to accentuate the delight.

The clay tones of party music sharpened and an old song began. A tangled scribble of vividly coloured memories materialised and George was taken back to his school leaver's disco. Not far away he noticed the bent face of Bob Frake, his old best friend at school. He was perched on the end of a chair, talking to the dark chiselled forms of Jack and Jo. Jo was Jack's wife. They were so alike.

George hadn't seen Bob Frake in years, only one time since leaving school. George had recently graduated, and he found Bob drinking a pale ale outside a country pub with some friends of his, sitting on an angular wooden bench and table that sported a wide white parasol. George was really happy to see Bob again. He'd meandered between three or four best friends in his last years of school, but Bob was the last. They were interested in the same nerdy, technical things, and had a similar attitude and hunger, but there was no competition between them. Never anything aggressive or jibey.

In the white sun, however, among the tossed spines of sandy grass that peppered the front of that pub, Bob didn't seem to care to see George that much. The few words felt awkward, and the short conversation didn't enter any emotional domain.

To George, the long pause hadn't ended their relationship. To Bob it had.

I suppose now, Pauline was George's best friend. He gulped down the last of his wine and mixed himself a gin and tonic. A glow of welcome relaxation spread from the crisp liquid on his tongue to his face and body beyond.

The pulsating music speaker was hooked to the wall in the distant corner of the front room, and next to it, filling the whole of the wall, was a lumbering drunken set of shelves, overfilled with weighty books on every subject, typically non-fiction or reference works. Many were unread. Adam loved these books, and right now he was on the tip of one foot stretching a thin arm up to a book that was tantalisingly out of reach. Next to him was the glowing cloud of 2me ("Two-me"), his favourite friend from school. 2me was a spirit entity, a child of infinite empathy who experienced everything in emotional terms. She and Adam were perfect companions. They found each other funny.

The rack of books quivered alarmingly. "Adam!" cried George across the humming room. "Careful!" Adam wheeled around, and George stepped over to steady the case. He took down the heavy book that Adam wanted. Wildlife photographs.

"You're sad." said 2me. Her glass voice was round and warm, rolling from silence and forming smooth, gentle waves. Her amorphous form was about the size of a beach ball and floating at head height. She was glowing with a green light that pulsed and flowed with each feeling and change in her thoughts and experiences. Like a flying magnet, she collected each emotion from those around her, living things, and feelings from places, objects, memories, and experiences, each alive and rich, but some greater than others depending on her focus and attention. At the moment she was thinking about George, and inside her nebulous form, lines of thought and antithought were flying in rapid curls, like screaming swifts, curls of sadness and curls of panic, joy and glory and escape, complexity, wonder, possibility, and destiny.

She pushed a bright glow from her inner being to her outer form, enjoying the pleasure of this emotion. George gulped his drink, and a ring of yellow rippled down 2me, a pulsation of sensation, the experience of the slight numbness that marks the first sign of intoxication.

Adam was sitting on the floor now, legs crossed and flicking too quickly through the pictures in the big book. Without looking up he spoke in his blunt monotone. "My dad's going to die." His eyes were locked on the book: Mammals, birds, amphibians, fish, reptiles, insects.

"I like parties!" said 2me with girlish glee. "That man's in love!" Her light pulsed an intense pink glow, so bright that it lit up the whole corner of the room. Her form stretched like a cat on sunny tiles, enjoying each arc of joy from this rare pleasure. She was referring to Bob, who had his back to the trio.

George finished his drink and felt like another. He filled his glass with a sweet, neat whiskey that someone had placed on the nest of tables nearby. The good quality single malt was a rare pleasure. He was enjoying the light feeling of letting go. He knew that he should really make the effort and talk to people, but he didn't want to. He wanted to do nothing, to forget the world and switch off for a night. He sat down on the floor and leaned up against the bookshelf next to his son.

Adam had stopped page turning and was looking at the cladogram with keen interest, the tree that showed each animal and its relation to every other species. This was his favourite page. It made everything explicit. There was a right place for everything, the whole world of living things scanned, marked and categorised.

2me came down to join them on the floor. George asked: "What's your favourite page, 2me?"

"I like all of them..." she said, then added "The ones with the pretty colours. Adam, show me the fish."

"No," said Adam firmly. He was following the paths of the animals with his wooden finger. Tracing the history from species, back, through aeons along the line of history to the bacteria.

"Don't be rude to 2me," said George, trying to be firm. He was feeling a little giddy. He poured another drink.

Adam couldn't empathise like other boys, so he didn't think it was rude to say what he wanted. He was incapable of imagining what it would be like to be someone else, to feel how they feel. To him he wasn't being rude, just confident.

"I don't mind," said 2me. She was pulsing yellow now, shaped like a fluffy star, a ball rippled with bump upon bump, translucent tennis-ball sized nodules that ebbed and exhaled. "I know he loves that page."

That's what made 2me wonderful. She had the power to feel the best in everyone because she truly understood them. Even a bad feeling was a good one when it was understood. She formed a ball and radiated beams of soft blue light. Around the ball a delicate halo teemed with glittering specks of vivid lilac.

George swallowed some more whiskey with a glunch and rested a tired arm on a raised single knee. He closed his eyes and leaned his head back on the wooden backbone of books, pushing into some small volumes to make a cave that was just the perfect size and the perfect comfort level for his body. Everything felt lovely. The music, the television, the tiny tick tap tap of knitting needles in the arthritic hands of his mother in law, his friends, his wife, his son.

He cracked opened a lazy eyelid and looked at Adam, his head down in fascinated gaze at his book, oblivious to the busy room. Behind the pie-slice hole in his chest, Adam's saw-blade heart turned excitedly. As the silver disc whirred, George thought he could see something written or drawn on it, a black shape that whizzed by, flick flick, almost too fast to see. Blink blink. It looked like a dinosaur.

George closed his eyes. A familiar pain in his head pulsed in knobbles, like 2me. He would be dead in a couple of weeks now but he didn't mind so much. He floated into sleep.

Chapter Ten

"Hello, sunshine!" rasped a familiar voice.

George lifted his head and found himself sitting and strapped into the oaken throne of the Gothic chapel. An icy breeze flowed over his bare arm. It romanced the flickering flame of the right hand torch on the opposite wall.

"Mister Vance, how nice of you to join us." His sibilants sliced through the air.

The thin interrogator was pacing, tip tap, in a small arc. His pale eyes with tiny pupils were fixed upon George. His bony arms were fixed behind his back. A black-gloved hand gripped the other with a tight squeak.

He spoke again: "Well, well. We're nearly there now."

He whipped out his arm and struck George across the face, causing his head to twist violently. George winced and leaned to the side, stretching his shoulders as far as his tight bonds would allow. A trickle of blood ran from his nostril.

"What did you do that for?" he gasped.

"No reason..." said the man. The guard backed away and continued to strut in front of his captor. He stretched his arms wide, twisting his wrists with a crick crack. He spoke again: "It's good for you. You might as well get used to it. Yes!"

He wheeled around rapidly and whipped George across his jaw with his leather riding strap. A lightning spark of pain shot through George's teeth, exploding spidery arms across his face, to his ear, then forming a dull ball of ache that lolled with each heartbeat. His head hung low.

"Sorry," said the unfeeling voice, "but it's all you have to look forward to now. This is your life, now."

George didn't want to listen. He was tired, but with fatigue comes relaxation, and peace. He lifted his heavy head, letting the pulsating flesh of his cheeks sag loosely.

The grey interrogator had stopped pacing and was looking at George calmly. George spoke: "I know I'm dying, but I don't care now. I don't care about the pain because I know it will end. I've done a lot in my life, done enough. I'll leave a wife and son and friends, my work, my machine, my research, my books. I could have done more, but I will leave the world a lot of great work and I will be remembered fondly."

The interrogator raised a slow eyebrow. "Pah!" He jumped up, and began to talk like a lawyer addressing an imaginary courtroom. "You might be remembered for a few weeks or months, or even years by some remote institutions..." He revved "remote" as though the word was an engine, "... but you will be forgotten soon enough. Everybody is. It's just a matter of time. The same is true of your work. Your importance is illusory. You're no more important than an ant, or something dead, a brick, an atom!"

With the deftness of a magician he rolled his crystal ball into view, holding it before George's gaze.

"Look!"

The mist cleared, and George saw a pulsating grey blob that looked soft, like a cell. Another blob appeared and fused with it, emitting a flash of blue-white light. More blobs appeared, and more flashes, faster and faster like a steam train running down an incline. Tiny specks of red light appeared, and whizzed around in orbit, carving curls of vivid lightning in spirals. More and more appeared until myriad specks became a cloud, then a vast sphere of light, expanding and growing like an atomic explosion, outwards, pushing a crisping boiling boundary into blackness. In the hive of this ball, new islands of light began to form as object attracted object, clustering together like driftwood meandering on the surface of a smooth river, cycling and waltzing, clumping and growing. At a critical point the objects ignited with a boom, shining out intense yellow sunlight, edged with crackling arcs of fire and nuclear ribbon. Jagged grey-black rocks tumbled, end over end, then smashed into each other, splitting into great shards of flint, shards which wheeled around in streams before curling back, pulled into masses, then growing hotter as they clustered tightly together, forming a lava ball, a sphere of molten rock. The ball cooled, revealing a cracked crust, splayed with lines of bright red fire, then a hiss as water appeared, spattering, and then covering the surface of this hot planet, rising and pulsating, growing into a vast salty ocean. Clouds of white ribbon shot towards the horizon, then mountains appeared, at first brown, and then green, and then buildings appeared, clay, wood, smoking, and black and white, then steel, and tiny people darting like excited ants. There was Pauline, but young, now a woman, their wedding, the party, now old, her wrinkled arm outside her soft bed embedded in its deep warm cover. Her hand went limp, dead. Now Trevor as an old man, bent and lumbering on a street, he clutches his chest and collapses, then George's mother's new grave, some fresh white lilies fall with a crump onto the brown soil, then the hand of rusting Adam. Opening, closing, creaking open, then still. Then an explosion and everywhere rubble, buildings destroyed and the surface of the Earth laid flat. The green of the mountains flashed into charred black. The oceans grew hot and pulled back, fizzing and sucked away into coughing, steaming puddles among a desert of cracks, the sky transformed from blue to red, and the burning orb of sun whipped and burst, spewing liquid nuclear fire across space. Stars burst like bubbles, and vast clouds of violet gas were pulled into thin wisps and then strings. Sharp tumbling rocks shattered. Dusty moons cracked as if cloven by gigantic axes, then were pulled apart, pulverised and ripped into columns of grey talcum powder that ran in helical strips of enormous length. The last globe of light was stretched into an ellipsoid and torn into blackness with a screaming pop, everything dark and pulled into elastic strings, thinner and thinner, and then the strings cracked, like a jigsaw puzzle smashed, irregular bits that tumbled smaller and smaller, darker and darker, folded and broken and drifting gently apart. Gently shrinking. Gently fizzing into tiny silver spheres, spheres that slowly blinked on and off. On and off. With gentle smoothness, the spheres became blue, twinkling clouds of vapour. The twinkles slowed and slowed and slowed, and then exhaled a final microscopic gasp of blue light.

"Even atoms will be forgotten," said the man. He withdrew the ball. "Nothing you do will last."

His argument was impeccable. A purpose to life was an illusion; but wait. The difference between an atom and a man is that a man can ponder this very question, and an atom cannot. The quality of purpose, the meaning of meaning, was something in the mind, and like anything there, it can be changed.

"Life," said George slowly, "has whatever meaning you want. If the only options are to strive to live as long as possible or die, then I choose to strive. It's more interesting, if nothing else. Existence is pleasurable. The experience of feeling, seeing, knowing. It's what makes a man better than an atom. Better than a hamster."

George was smiling. The guard was standing to one side, stroking his chin. Brushing and caressing his lips with the tips of his fingers.

"A somewhat... hedonistic viewpoint," he said, pensively. "Your only purpose has become survival, just as mine is to kill you. How meaningless. How selfish! See, here!"

He unveiled the ball once more. In the centre was a desiccated yellow eye with a shrivelled dark iris, malformed like a chewed metal washer. It blinked.

"That is the last intelligent eye to ever see. A true master of survival. He lives not for himself but for another."

The scene faded into a blur, then reformed into a face, someone George knew, or thought he knew. His mother..? Yes, this felt like his mother. In his chest a globule of liquid love appeared and spread briefly through his body.

The guard pocketed the ball and spoke more slowly: "Perhaps there is yet hope."

He turned away, arms wide and fingers spread, swimming in the cold air of the stone chamber. He moved towards the red velvet curtain that draped loosely over the opposite wall, and dramatically pulled it aside. It dropped to the floor in a crumple of crimson folds. In the wall behind were two arched doors, both heavy wood and pitted with diamond shaped iron studs. The left one was painted white, the other black. Each had a large metal hoop for a handle.

"One is life, the other death," he announced. "The only question," he added with a mischievous grin, "is whether you can reach the doors before I kill you!"

The man darted forwards and shoved something into George's mouth, pressing it in with the flat of his gloved hand. It had the acid taste of a rubber balloon, scrunched into a creased ball. With a vice grip the interrogator held George's head back, covering his eyes and began to pump with the other hand, inflating the balloon. Each pump sent a pulse of pain through the side of George's head, a shock of ache that grew and grew, bigger and bigger with each hard push. His only sensation was the regular throb of his headache. Throb. Throb. Throb.

Chapter Eleven

George gasped, and opened his eyes with a shock, to a gentle daylight that filtered in through his bedroom window. The soft fresh feather duvet crisped above his sweating arms. His head was pounding. He shouldn't have drunk anything last night, especially with pain killers. He scrunched his fingers around his eyes, and then round in spirals on his temples, then sat up in the yellow covers.

A glance in the oval mirror opposite showed a pale, thin face. His dark hair was the shape of a cluster of young witches dancing in the woods. He flattened it with his hands and leaned out of the right side of the bed with a groan, then fumbled at the space under the bed for a plastic bottle of water that he liked to stash there. The pulsing whoosh in his ears matched his headache. His fingertips, and then splayed palms, enjoyed the feel of the deep woollen carpet. He found the bottle and sat up to take a welcome swig of cold tap water.

Strange that he should see his mother again, in the orb. He hadn't thought about her in years. Her name was Delilah. Her maiden name was Gertelbaum. Delilah Gertelbaum. Her parents were Austrian Jews but George knew them only from browny photographs that used to be black and white. Thick rimmed glasses, long heavy coats, buns of hair, smoking pipes, smart suits with pocket-watch chains.

She was a depressive, and Rothko did at least as much around the house as his wife, but they all shared the jobs. George loved his mother enormously, but he never thought that she felt the same, and her apathetic, or cruelly honest, responses to his childhood drawings and stories hurt him more than she seemed to realise. George was living away at college when his father died, and despite weekend visits, his mother was largely left to herself. When George went to university he hardly ever went home, and while he was in his first year he read the unexpected news that Delilah had left with a carpet salesman and gone to live with him in Australia. She was still there now, as far as George knew. At least he hadn't heard otherwise. He hadn't had a word from her since then... no actually he had, once. An unexpectedly lovely letter written to him when he got married. George meant to reply but didn't get around to it.

Her address, or the carpet salesman's address, was around the house somewhere, some odd sounding little town like Woolamunga, or something like that. Maybe this was the right time to write? Yes, it was just the right time. Writing might even help George. She didn't even know about Adam.

But wait! George didn't need to write. He could use his machine to visit her in an instant. What an amazing thought. He had the ultimate doorway in his basement and could use it to find out about his family, about anyone. He could even use it to visit his dead grandparents... except that he couldn't speak

Austrian, or German, rather. Hmm, maybe not. But visiting his mother was the perfect idea.

Enthused by this new idea, George unwrapped himself out of bed and got dressed in new morning clothes. He pulled back the light yellow curtains and looked out, peering through the leafy branches at the new day. It was slightly overcast, but still bright and warm, and cloudless in the distance, like the embodiment of hope. The window was ajar, propped open just a crack, and the summer smells seemed to wash away every brown particle of hangover. He stepped to the bedside table and slid open a wooden drawer with a squeak. He took out a couple of pain killers and gulped them down with a good measure of water. "Breakfast first," he thought, and then he would go and meet his mother. The prospect felt exciting.

He jogged down the stairs, creaking the bannister, and swung towards the kitchen. Some party detritus decorated the room, stacked plates with flaky remains on the stocky pine table, and a scatter of cakes, now sheltered under a light canopy of cling film.

He filled the kettle with a slosh and clicked it on, popping a tea bag into a mug, and tapping a silver teaspoon down in anticipation. Nobody seemed to be around. It was Saturday morning, so Pauline would have taken Adam swimming.

They hadn't returned by the time George had finished his oak-smoked bacon, mushrooms, and fried bread breakfast. He was in the basement now, the cavern of eternal night, eternally lit by humming strips of yellow green. He was at his desk, perched on the front edge of his office chair, gaze locked on the flat blue screen of his computer, its face, the gateway to its soul. His mother's address wasn't here. It wasn't a serious problem, he would use the normal search. He stood up, and wheeled the chair neatly beneath the desk.

Fed, watered, medicated, clean, well dressed. George was prepared for a journey this time. "Computer," he said, "I want to go to my mother, Delilah Vance."

The array of whirring fans inhaled with the joy of a new task. Lights danced and soon, and without drama, the titanium blue voice of the machine said: "Target located."

"Open gateway."

The room beyond the disc of the trans-dimensional gateway had hard, white walls, and an olive, linoleum floor. An ugly metal coat hanger, skeletal white wire, like a frightening relic from a Romanian orphanage, was visible. A clean white coat dangled from it. The ceiling was too high to see through the iris. George stepped through. A faint bleach smell permeated the air of this undoubtedly hospital room. A bed made of sturdy tubular steel was next to the wall. It was on large grey castors like a shopping trolley. At its feet was a rickety table on wheels scattered with small boxes, and a snakey chromium tool. There was a heavy radiator on one wall, next to an alarming plaque that dictated the correct procedure in case of a fire. The ceiling was tiled with square speckled tiles in buff. One tile was loose, ajar. The next tile was missing, a dark hole that led to the inner biology of this clinic. The solitary door was opposite, light brown and windowless, with the bar of a tubular brushed metal handle on the left, ready to be pulled. Next to it was the coat stand.

George turned around and saw that the portal had opened in a wall, over a large mirror the size of a door. He took a pace and rubbed his hands. The coat was too tempting and he tried it on, enjoying the instant feeling of medical superiority and realising that the freedom of the wide flapping coat, like the cloak of a king, was definitely contributing towards it. "Mum must be nearby," he thought.

He grabbed the handle and entered a hospital corridor, long, and lined with doors. There was the back of a lumbering patient in the distance, and nobody else. He moved to his left to the brightly coloured sign that was barred to the ceiling.

Midwifery left. Child and Adolescent Unit left. Mental Heath right. Exit right. Main Reception up.

Then he noticed the dark door opposite. There was a rectangular aluminium frame on it, and the white card inside had 'Delilah Vance' written on it in blue ink. He stepped forwards and took the handle, using some force to push the door and overcome the heavy piston of the automatic closing system that each of these doors had. He was ready to say something like "Hello mum," or "Surprise!", but it was he that was surprised. His mother was on top of the bed in a white gown, heavily pregnant and apparently in labour, and young, and beautiful.

"Hello doctor," she panted. "That was quick. They're happening all of the time now."

"Oh, erm," said a stunned George before inanely asking: "How are you?"

"In pain!" was the cross reply.

George immediately felt out of his depth, and felt like he looked out of his depth. Suddenly the door flew open and his father burst in, dragging a train of a midwife and a doctor with him. "Now then, relax Mrs. Vance," said the doctor.

"Everything is going to be all right."

George stepped back and cowered next to the door, watching everything from a safe distance. An anxious looking Rothko went around to the back of the bed and sat next to his wife on the spongy leatherette of a small metal chair.

The doctor was pumping a blood pressure machine, its black rubber blanket wrapped around Delilah's arm.

"Is this your first?" enquired the midwife.

"Yes," burst Rothko.

This wasn't what George had expected when he wanted to see his mother again. To be here at his own birth. He couldn't say anything, not ask her about her life so far, or tell her about his. He couldn't seek to build a bond, or make a bond, or anything. All he could do was stand in a corner and watch. Watch the woman giving birth. She did look different though, so different from how he remembered her. She was hardly the woman he knew at all. None of the weight or sadness, none of the knocks and scars that carve a child into an adult shape over a lifetime. Her hair was bubbled with curls like he'd never seen, and her face so young. Younger than he was now. Younger than Pauline when he met her. Rothko was different too, middle aged but looking fitter than he remembered, perched quivering on the tip of the tiny chair, not very different from the teenage rebel he'd met in heaven. Delilah winced with a transient pain and reached for Rothko's concerned hand. Then she squeezed it and smiled at him, and gave him such a look of love and joy that George felt overwhelmed with emotion. Overwhelmed with the love and innocence of this young girl that he hadn't seen before. George suddenly felt guilty that he thought her cold. Guilty and sad that he had thought her loveless, had blamed her for his childhood loneliness, when right now she was filled with more love than he had ever felt for her.

He closed his wet eyes and leaned back, feeling the cold plaster of the wall behind him for a few moments. Then he slid quietly out of the noisy room, down the hard corridor and into the small square room from which he entered.

The portal, though still circular, looked like a mirror and not his basement. He stepped towards it and hesitantly extended his arm towards the glass. It went right through. The gateway was clearly still active. He gingerly stepped though but, oddly, didn't find himself in his basement.

At first he thought he'd entered a new room in the hospital. A similar room of the same size, with the same doorway, but it was no reflection. The shiny olive linoleum floor of the old room had gone, now replaced with a smooth, dull white surface. The edge of the floor, where it touched the wall, bent up in a gentle curve to touch walls, coated with white paint that had a vaguely iridescent copper sheen. The fire warning was still there though, and the heavy radiator, as before, but with different paint. The wheeled bed was gone, replaced with a black sofa of sorts, a metal frame of angular tubes with piston-like cross braces, topped with a spongy pillow surface wrapped in a black Hessian-type material. The skeletal coat hanger was there, unchanged. The ceiling tiles were unchanged too, although there was no hole.

Intrigued, George decided to explore. He noticed that he was still wearing the long white gown, and decided to leave it on. He left the room and found himself in the same corridor, lit by fluorescent square ceiling lights that reflected in the same polished floor. There were no people. George turned towards the sign, still suspended from the ceiling but now different. The writing was different, and a tiny white light shone onto the letters to make them easier to read.

Cardiac Rehab. left. Child and Adolescent Unit left. Mental Heath right. Exit right. Main Reception up.

He couldn't help but look at the door opposite, the one to his mother's room. The same aluminium frame was stuck in the same place. The black typed lettering inside now read 'George Vance'. A shiver ran through him.

He had to know what was beyond. He stepped forward and opened the door to the tiny room he had occupied only moment ago. The same, creaking metal-framed bed, the bed his mother was lying in, was there. Lying in the bed he saw himself, unconscious. Frail. His head was bandaged with white bonds and curling wires of yellow and blue were spiralling from beneath the cloth, connected to a large machine that showed a screen of scribbling, darting lines. A wider, ribbed tube came from his mouth, connected to a transparent box that was breathing using two bellows, one black and one white, that moved up and down in a regular rhythm. A soothing hissy rhythm of up, and down. Up, and down. A tube was taped inside his nose that ran to a milky food source. His grey, bony left hand rested on top of the neatly folded white linen sheet. A hose ran from it to a drip that hung beside the bed on a vertical pole, watching over the sleeping patient. A cardiac machine was beside the bed, where Rothko's metal chair had sat. Its tiny display showed a graph of the patient's beating heart; large numbers showed the rate, and a cute little love-heart symbol periodically flashed. The pulse was slow.

There was nobody here. Nobody except George, the traveller,

looking at George the patient.

Suddenly, a red light lit on the heart machine and an electronic siren wailed in two-tone. The lines on the brain machine scribbled furiously in a chaotic rabble, as though drawing graphs of the paths of pebbles and lumps of rock that tumble and collapse in a landslide. The electrocardiograph continued to wail. The number showed zero. The tone a steady beep. The cute little heart wasn't there. George was in a panic, unsure what do to. Heart massage? The kiss of life? But all of these machines in the way! Panic! He opened the door and stared left, and right, and ahead, down the corridors. Nobody! There was nobody here! Why wasn't there anybody here!?

He turned back into the room. The bellows sank, releasing their air with a melancholic sigh. The lines on the graph were flat. The landslide was over. The pale hand of the patient twitched slightly, ever so slightly, like the last performance by a dreaming pianist. Then rest. Stillness. A constant wailing from the cardiac machine. An electronic lament.

The traveller leaned heavily on the handle and left the room in shock. Where was Pauline? Where was Adam? Where was anybody? Not even a doctor was there. Not even a plant, or a warm wish. He slipped off the white gown and it fell from his shoulders into a soft pile, onto the hard floor outside the room

George was born in, the same room in which he would die.

He stepped slowly towards home. Back along the corridor and into the small room with the metal bed and the faded fire emergency instructions. The back wall showed his basement now, a perfect disc as wide as his arms could stretch. The hole that had cut through space and time, connecting his present with his past, and his future.

But the future wasn't set, and no future could ever be certain. It wasn't certain that he would die alone. Alone, apart from himself, the helpless, hapless observer. His knowledge of the future had already changed the path of fate.

He stepped briskly through the portal and quickly slid open the top draw of his sleek aluminium desk. He pulled out a sharp knife with a thin blade in sections that could be snapped off. He extended the blade with a push of his thumb, raised his left hand and drew the knife gently across the back of it, slicing a fine line. A thin, straight line. A line to make a scar that was not on the hand of the man he had just seen die.

He was not going to die alone, and not now, not soon. He had had enough of coming to terms with his so-called fatal disease. He didn't want to live forever, just longer. As long as possible. He was not going to die soon. He was not ready and not going to give in. Not yet. Somewhere out there, in the vast panoply of time and space, is the answer, and he, he George Vance, would find it.

"Close gateway," he commanded, then: "Find me the owner of that last eye, the master of survival. Find me the longest lived man in the universe."

Chapter Twelve

There was a sound like a thunderclap. A deep dark rumble that pounded and shook through George and through the room, running like a tsunami, as though the building had been lifted by giant invisible hands and cast down in anger. George fell from his feet and landed on the floor with a hard clatter, banging his side on the desk as he went.

The bank of computers on the opposite wall blew out a warm air, throbbing with each rotation of the fan blades inside. The pulses increased as more fans were engaged, more power drained, hotter and hotter grew the circuits as more and more resources were pulled by the great brain. More energy, sucked along the thick black rubber cables that squirmed along the floor of the basement like great robotic tentacles.

The air began to heat up, and the sickly smell of warm silicon began to flow from the slatted vents that lined the angular edges of the monolithic electronic brains. The red lights danced and ran, round and square, darting, flying, fetching and carrying information, tripping, trapping, faster and faster, until every red light was lit. The outer ring of the gateway then began to flicker with light, tiny white specks at the finger-wide gap that separated the thin inner ring of copper hair from the hard steel lump of the large one. There was a zissing flash, and a vomit of sparks. The matrix of ceiling lights flickered nervously and then began to flash, mirroring the red lights on the computer.

The cold voice spoke in a damaged tone: "Connecting."

George was cowering near his desk. Should he abort? Should he wait? He flexed his sore hand and licked the dripping blood. He paused.

"Computer," he spoke clearly.

The room was shaking. The computer's voice began to gabble disconnected consonants, searching for a word, a phrase. "G-g-g-g. B-b-b. Go-go-gop."

"Computer!" he shouted.

"Hope a hope a hope a," said the computer, round and round like the cards that flap and tick in the wheel of a crashed bicycle. "Openo peno peno pen..."

George clambered to his feet, hauling himself up with help from the thick, vibrating surface of the desk. The power supply was on the other side of the room, in a dark mass of cables under the stairs, a black cave of thick liquorice wires. The main power was controlled by a knife switch in there, a great handle installed in an homage to Baron Victor von

Frankenstein. George fixed his eyes upon the handle.

"Open gateway," said the voice, and all became silent. A pause. There was a fizzle, and the tiny blue dots that began the gate opening process materialised in the ring of the great machine. They ran and ran, shot, sliced. There was a white disc, and then there it was. The gate was open. The basement was still again. The fans of the great ranks of computers whirred gently back to idle. The last red dot glowed, and then faded away to rest in its peace.

George exhaled, and wiped another line of wet blood from his hand. He moved closer to take a look at the scene beyond the portal.

Before him was a vast indoor expanse with a steely grey floor and ceiling, tiled with rigid hexagons. The distant wall, visible through a forest of columns or caskets, was concave as though the room were circular, and made of the same metal, panelled in sections and edged with tiny rivets. The air that flowed through the portal was cool and fresh, smelling of an ice box, or a crisp Alpine morning.

George stepped though. It was a warehouse by the looks of things, and the columns were boxes and containers, square and cylindrical, made of plastic and metal, of different sizes and heights. These were stacked and placed around the room in a neat symmetrical patten as if they had grown there. The light came from orbs, glowing green, and set into the ceiling like cowering eggs. There were no windows, but there was a single door with rounded corners and a circular porthole, ahead. There were no signs of life.

George moved towards the door, clanking over the curious metal flooring like an astronaut. He peered through the circular window into a brightly lit room arrayed with hissing pipes and machines fronted with brass wire grills. Still no sign of life. The door had no obvious knob, but there was a red metal flap, a bit like the handle inside a car door. He pulled it and the door slowly slid to the side, rumbling into the metal wall with a grinding sound. He stepped though. He was at the tip of a crescent, a short hallway, that curled left and around beyond sight. The sweeping wall opposite was a window, a wide, curving window with rounded corners that looked out into the black and silver curtain of outer space. George took a step forwards, eyes locked in awe on the beautiful starscape, and discovered that he had entered a large chamber, a domed room lined with ancient looking computers that flashed and hummed. Snakes of brass tubing, desks scattered with myriad paper fragments, machine parts, glowing display panels, and all manner of detritus were piled up into quivering towers.

"Who are you?" grated a startled metal voice with an Italian accent. For the first time George noticed something move, a metallic, cylindrical object like a oil drum. With a hop, this curious thing bounced backwards on a solitary mechanical leg. Out of top of the drum poked the shoulders and head of a shrivelled man, a man cast in flesh made of ribbons of wrinkles and lumps, like a human walnut. His yellow cheekbones protruded like hard islands in a liquid sea of folded skin, a skin marked with large brown blotches and occasional wiry white hairs that spiralled and twisted like dancers petrified by the gaze of Medusa. His leathery ears were enormous, twisted and asymmetrical, fringed with lugs and pits like jigsaw puzzles. Black pipes ran from their hairy middles, plugging into an unseen port in the back of his metal torso. His right eye was closed in a sunken blue-black pit. The other was open, its dry, yellow cornea surrounding an angular lumpy iris. This was the eye that George had seen in the crystal ball.

"How did you get here?" said the voice. The man's tight thin lips did not move. The voice came from a metal box that seemed to be embedded into his throat. Below that was his drum-like chest, from which two mechanical arms protruded, black ribbed and terminating in shiny metal pincers.

"My name is George. I've come using my machine, a trans-dimensional gateway. I'm..."

"Wait!" snapped the voice. His left pincer swished upwards and deftly flicked a switch on his chest. The voice gargled on: "Sorry, I had turned my ears off. I am deaf without my machine."

The man rotated his iron body towards George with a swish, and hopped forwards on a foot like a rubber plunger. "I apologise for my appearance. I am very old and the years have not been kind." The man's eye opened wide for a moment, looking into the air to a distant memory.

George was a little frightened by this monstrous sight, but for all of the horror of his appearance, the face up-close looked soft and the voice seemed friendly, polite, somehow familiar.

The man spoke "I am the great Arturo Imbroglione."

"My computer brought me here," said George. "I have a brain tumour. I'm dying. I'm looking for a cure... do you... might you know of a cure?"

The man cocked his head to one side. "A brain tumour..." spoke the robotic voice, now more hushed: "Yes. I can cure you. My wife..." Those words seemed to spark a poignant memory in the man, "she has a brain tumour too." He became more alert, and then smiled with enthusiasm. "Come, look! I can show you so much!"

Arturo turned energetically and hopped to the back of the room with a regular whizz clunk, whizz clunk, as he bounded up and down on the wide rubbery plate that was his foot. George followed him, around a vertical column, and into a concave crevice like a cramped office, containing a brown desk that was surrounded on three sides by arcs of shelves that reached the ceiling, piled high with overflowing papers, books, ornaments, machines, pinned notes, pens and probes on curly wires, glass balls, jars filled with gloopy pickled things that were impossible to make out, and all manner of mechanical clutter. The desk was rounded, and itself piled with books, papers, devices, and the same detritus, but there was a clear patch in the middle. Just above it was a glass dome resting on an embossed copper base. Through the dome George could see a large brown moth. It was not moving.

"It is dead," said Arturo. He extended his arms with a motorised buzz, and with unexpected gentleness lifted the dome and took out the moth, waving it towards George: "Here."

George held out an uncomfortable hand and felt the soft body. He didn't want to touch the furry thing, but he felt unable to refuse. It was pretty. He looked at the brown patterns on the wings. Black, brown, and tan. Rings within rings, like the end of a log.

Arturo took the moth and placed it back under the dome. "Now, watch."

He flicked a switch on the outer rim of the copper base and the glass of the dome lit up with a white light. Slowly, the metal floor beneath the moth began to glow as though hot.

"Life is energy," said Arturo, "Entropy. Information. All information deteriorates, eventually, but in the short term it can be tricked, sucked from one area to another."

The wings of the moth began to move, slowly. Down like the first stretch of stiff old bones, then up, more loosely. The antennae shuddered, the first lightning spark of an awakening brain. A leg jerked, and the moth leaped, flying in a frantic flicker against the walls of the glass dome. Trapped, but alive.

"All of my life I've been searching," said Arturo wistfully. He creaked an aged neck towards George and peered at him with narrow eyes. Then, pulled from his thoughtful state, he extended a right pincer to flick the switch beneath the dome, turning off its light. The moth continued to struggle against the invisible walls of his prison.

George was impressed by this display: "Could it work with a human?"

"Yes..." said Arturo thoughtfully. "Wait!" He became more animated, and wheeled his metal hips to the side, then hopped further back into the depths of this room, to a distant wall and a second alcove stacked with more shelves, hand tools, and devices plugged with spaghetti wires of black and red that cascaded downwards in swinging loops. Arturo clamped his pincers onto a brown rectangular box and hopped back. A metal thumb depressed a switch on the box and it hummed with a rapid pulse, shining a column of blue light filled with glittering droplets, like dust caught in headlights. He shone the beam through the dome onto the moth. Glowing yellow particles, infinitely tiny, began to coalesce on the flapping wings of the creature, brightest at the tips and falling away with each beat, sucked upwards, through the glass and towards the brown box. The moth stopped beating and sat down, flapping more slowly as the stream of peppering-fire ran from moth to box. The wings slowed yet more. There were far fewer particles now, cast into the air with each sweeping beat, and pulled towards the humming box like a magnet. After a short time the wings stopped moving. A final cluster of glowing specks formed on the furry antennae of the moth and then leaped into the air, diving into the invisible flowing river of life that ran from the moth, through the wall of the thick glass prison, through space and into the mouth of the small brown device.

Click. The machine was turned off. The moth lay still. Arturo spoke: "This machine extracts information."

While the machine was humming, George had become aware of a familiar pain. A dull ache that radiated from the side of his head and down through his neck to glow across his body.

A dry, cardboard voice suddenly spoke from the distant end of the room: "Arturo, my love!" George leaned back and took a step to see better. The end corner of the room was a cluttered pile of antiques. There was a short section of wall next to the end of the sweeping space-window, and upon it hung lots of photographs and paintings in dusty, gilded frames. In the corner, stood a pile of floor-standing shelves made from polished walnut wood, shelves piled with antiques; a brass lamp, a leathery black camera, and women's shoes cluttered at the bottom. Next to this was a small wooden octagonal table with fine curling legs that led to neat claw-ball feet. On top of the table was an old gramophone with a wide paper horn in golden hues. Beside it was a red velvet curtain, draped over a section of wall. There was nobody visible. From the reedy quality of the sound George was convinced that the voice came from the gramophone horn.

Arturo said "Excuse me. That is my wife," then towards the end of the room: "Coming, my love!"

He hopped away with a clunking rhythm, leaving George filled with thoughts, overwhelmed by this place and the bizarre little robot man.

This place was incredible, eccentric, ancient. Filled with the massed relics of a long life. The books ranged from classical literature to specialised volumes on science and technology. George scanned the volumes, then noticed a name. Surely not, could it be? He twisted his head to one side to read "Overcoming Muscular Dystrophy in Six Short Weeks by Roger Castavet." - his next door neighbour.

He slid out the volume and accidentally pulled with it a thin yellow envelope which tumbled to the ground. He bent down, embarrassed. Under the table, beneath the dome, he saw some of the workings of the machine above, some brassy gears, moving parts, a belt of rubber or cloth that to his scientific brain looked like a Van der Graaf Generator, a machine for making static electricity. He pondered for a moment on how this could be involved in restoring life.

He lifted the familiar looking envelope. It was a packet of sunflower seeds like the one David Prentiss had given him, except that "Fake" was written on the front in black marker pen. He held the translucent envelope up to the light and shook it. The shadowed contents looked like buttons. Curious.

He stood up and put the packet carefully on the desk, then flicked through the paperback book. It wasn't a medical book but a writer's guide, an instruction manual on how to be an author. There was a card between the pages, hidden deep inside like a secret bookmark. It was a photograph.

"Yes..." said the metallic voice, surprising him from behind: "I was young, once."

George looked at the photograph. Black and white. A smart young man with a flick-flick of a black moustache, in a black tail-suit and a silk top hat, standing next to a glamorous woman in a long glittering dress of white. They looked like a couple of nineteen-thirties film stars. The man looked like Bob Frake, George's old school friend. He looked at the back. "The Great Imbroglione" was written there in curling handwriting.

Arturo continued: "I love my wife. Still, after all of these years. At first it was joy, the warmth, the fun and companionship and sex. The pleasure of attraction and finding just the right

The Many Beautiful Worlds...

person, what we felt was exactly right. After a year or two the fire had faded but the compatibility was still there, the need, and understanding. There would always be a pleasure, a transient pleasure from someone new or something, some distracting desire, but the greatest love is a long term accord. A mapping of two similar brains so that each is accustomed to the other. So accustomed to the other that separation becomes impossible."

Arturo hopped to the velvet curtain and pulled it aside on its brass rail. "Here she is."

George stepped closer. In the dim recess beyond was a cylindrical glass tank containing the upright naked body of a young woman, suspended in a greenish sea-water fluid. Long strands of red hair waved and curled in the meandering current. Gurgling bubbles permeated her watery environment.

"She died of a brain tumour on the day we were married," he said with a distinctly sad tone, "but she will live forever within me." Arturo blinked away a small tear from his solitary eye, and gazed in awe at the floating body in the tank. He raised an arm and tapped the glass with a cold metal hand, the iron fingers rapping the surface in a sad homage to touch.

"...I live for you..." said the gramophone in its thin, grey voice.

George peered through the watery murk at the peaceful face beyond the glass. Next to the soft young features of the sleeping beauty, on the left side on her head, among the drifting strands of hair, was a road of fine copper wires that curled in arcing strands before embedding into the left side of her skull, piercing her white skin and penetrating into her brain.

A spark of pain shot through George's head, emanating from that same point. He dropped the book with a clatter and clawed the left side of his head, dragging his fingers back through his hair. "You said you could help me... my tumour. Please, will you help?"

Then George noticed something moving. There was a record on the gramophone, turning. Slowly, but rotating and glinting periodically in the light.

Arturo was still looking adoringly at the face of the woman in the jar, his metal hand stroking the smooth glass gently. "Emotions are transient but an intelligent belief will last forever," he said, "When you understand that, love becomes immortal."

"I will always love you," said the gramophone, "Love you, love you, love you..."

The needle had become stuck. The woman wasn't alive, it was an act. This whole place was a set up. A trick! A delusion! "The Great Imbroglione". A magician - of course! The old photograph, Houdini's tank, the moth! "See here, members of the audience! See how the volunteer confirms that the moth is dead! Gaze in wonder as I restore it to life!"

Pound, pound, pound went George's head, now swirling, like boiling soup. Duped. Shocked. Ashamed. Angry. Panic!

A light-bulb switched on in his mind, a terrible, lucid flash of truth. Truth, that most horrific, that most unavoidable class of information. There is no escape!

George cast his flailing arm aside, sending the gramophone tumbling to the ground, shattering the disc, smashing the box, and causing a cascade of antiques from the smart wooden shelves that tumbled and crashed down with the sound, and hopelessness, of a piano falling down a mountain.

He turned and fled, clanking vast strides along the metal decking, past the moth in its glass dome, past the sweeping window that showed the spotlights of stars, the million distant eyes of a laughing audience, laughing at the show. He must get home. Home to his wife. Home to his friends. Home to his love. Home. Home. Home!

He ripped at the door control and burst into the black icy air of the warehouse. Forwards, between the dark columns of boxes, of props, old cases splashed with bill posters of music halls, domed arenas, jaded brown theatres, and fake plastic television sets. From this delusion he ran, and out, through the gateway, to his basement, and home.

"Close gateway." he said. He looked sideways, eyes fixed on the cave of black cables, the home of the main power supply. Inside was the knife switch: twin chromium blades separated by a black wooden handle now down, locked, fixed in the 'on' position. "Enough!" he said. Enough of travelling, of escape, of tricks and avoidance.

He inhaled. Blood was coming from his nostril. He wiped it with his knuckle, then clambered over the thick, hard tentacles of cable, bent low to enter the cavern beneath the stairs, grasped the switch firmly, and lifted it, slamming it into the vertical position. The computers went off and a cloak of blackness enveloped the basement. In the dark, the whirling hum of the ever-cooled machines started to wind down. The air purification fans free-wheeled as they relaxed, turning slower and slower, quieter and quieter, until eventually there was only silence and stillness.

Chapter Thirteen

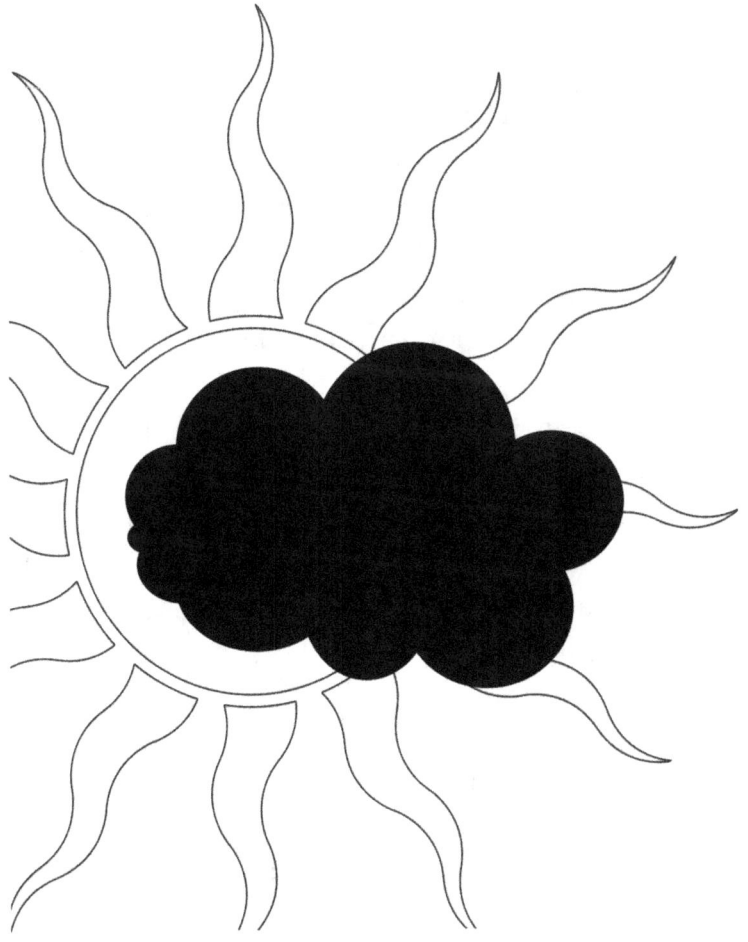

George gulped, and rested in the darkness for a few minutes, leaning his cheek against the warm body of a thick trunk of cable. From the depths of the under-stairs cave he emerged, crawling slowly in complete darkness, around the corner, groping for the foot of the stairs. He found the bottom step and walked up, emerging into the hall of the lit and independently powered house above.

There was a crackling sound, coming through the open kitchen door, and George leaned forwards to look in. A man in a suit then strode past in a daze, oblivious to George, and headed for the living room carrying a plate of sausage rolls. It was Trevor from work looking dreadfully sad. George couldn't ever recall seeing Trevor so emotional before.

George wheeled right, towards the front room. It was busy with dark-suited men and women in black dresses. The first person he saw was his wife, weeping and being embraced by David Prentiss. She had her back to George, her skin visible through a translucent panel on this, her least revealing black dress. He extended an arm to touch her shoulder. "What's up, love?" he enquired.

Pauline turned with a look of casual recognition and fought to blink away tears from her red eyes. "I can't believe he's dead." she sputtered, then turned back to the big arms of David, the television gardener. He patted her back. "She's very upset," said David in his west-country tones.

Down, immediately to George's left, Ursula was sitting in her favourite chair, dressed in a heavy black dress with a veil that wouldn't have looked out of place on Queen Victoria. She was knitting something with black wool and staring at the flickering television. The screen was showing a church service, with soft-focus close-ups of choir boys singing *Morning Has Broken* interleaved with bowed-head priests and the amassed relatives. Ursula addressed George sternly, continuing to knit automatically: "It's your fault he's dead, he was so much better than you!" Her eyes then re-locked onto the television.

George was beginning to feel worried. Behind David, in the middle of the room, he saw Adam, unusually dressed in a neat white shirt and black tie. Kneeling next to him and talking to him was the sympathetic Doctor Price. George moved closer and the doctor looked up with a warm smile. Adam turned around with glee, sending his metal heart spinning. "Doctor Price is telling me about intracranial malignant neoplasms!" he beamed.

The doctor responded to George "They absorb anything at this age don't they? He's quite a wonderful boy!" Then, addressing Adam: "Now Adam, What are the primary consequences of intracranial hypertension?"

"Vomiting?" enquired Adam.

George swallowed a queasy gulp of saliva. He was distracted by a light from the left. It was 2me, glowing violet in a spiralling swirl like a cloud made of wool. Beams and rods of light were curling in towards her centre and out, twisting and writhing like fighting biplanes. Her lower half was dark, and thick and damp, and large droplets of water were forming and raining onto the carpet in a steady, regular drum. Cute little hiccup sounds were coming from her. She was crying.

"Are you alright, 2me?" said George to the girl. He extended a hand to touch the warm candyfloss head of her barely corporeal mist. She blubbed: "Everyone is so sad. So lovely. This feeling is so strong, so powerful. So beautiful!"

With that, she radiated beams in all directions and became bright yellow, shining a feeling of great emotion, great joy and sadness. George was feeling quite overcome. Then he saw that behind 2me, near the back of the room where the food table had been, was a coffin, an open coffin of light wood with a white silk lining. With trepidation he moved towards the casket, eyes fixed, unable to blink. As he got closer he could see it was the body of a man. The face was Roger's. He was wearing a suit like George's, and lying peacefully as though he had casually fallen asleep and would awaken at any moment.

"Such a good man," quivered a weeping man's voice. It was Bob Frake, who looked up from the opposite side of the coffin. He clutched his face, covering his tearful eyes with his fingers. His voice continued: "He was so kind. Everybody loved him. Why did he have to die?"

George grasped the side of his face with his cold hand. His head was pounding, swimming. The darkness of closing his eyes seemed to help. He needed darkness, needed quiet. What were all these people doing here? What was going on?

He turned and covered his aching eyes with his palms, clutching at his forehead. The room was spinning. He felt sick and began to vomit. His legs felt weak and gave way beneath him, plunging him forwards and into a crunching pile. He heard Pauline scream and the voice of Doctor Price shout: "Somebody call an ambulance!"

Darkness.

Chapter Fourteen

George slowly creaked open his sticky eyes. He saw a blurred shape: his hand. The air that blew over its skin felt icy. He was lying face down on a hard floor. It was plastic, yet it looked like rough stone cobbles. He bent his neck up and exhaled, sending a cloud of surface dust tumbling away. He was on the floor of the Gothic stone chapel. He twisted left and right, casting a wide glance over the imitation stones. There was no sign of the interrogator. He pushed down with both hands and climbed to his feet. He was indeed alone.

The heavy chair was there, behind him and to his side. The brown leather restraints were open, hanging loose. A bright white light above him was casting stark shadows. He turned and blinked at the intensity of the beam, a hot spotlight. He raised his hand to shield his eyes. There were more lights here, two, heavy, floor-standing spotlights on tall metal poles stood behind the chair at its opposite corners.

There was no back wall behind the chair, just black space. He cowered beneath the cone of light and squinted into the darkness. He couldn't make out a distant wall, but it felt as though he were inside a vast warehouse. Beneath the skeletal spotlight leg, on a robust pyramidal base, was a film camera, its head sagging, dead, vacant. Around the floor lay a tangle of electrical cables, and to the right, exactly behind the oaken throne there was a small folding chair with a canvas seat. A loose pile of white paper lay on it. He moved to it and picked it up. "INT: GOTHIC CHAMBER – NIGHT" it said.

GEORGE is strapped to a heavy wooden chair. INTERROGATOR is close to him.

INTERROGATOR
Open your eyes. Come on!
(grasps GEORGE'S hair)
Wakey wakey.

GEORGE
Agh!

INTERROGATOR
That's better!

...

The script of his torture. He flicked to another page...

INTERROGATOR
Even atoms will be forgotten.
Nothing you do will last.
(pause)

GEORGE
Life has whatever meaning you want.
If the only options are to strive to live
as long as possible or die, then I choose
to strive...

...

He paused for a moment's thought, then flicked through to the
last page.

GEORGE collapses. PAULINE screams and faints, caught by
DAVID PRENTISS.

DOCTOR PRICE
Somebody call an ambulance!

FADE TO:

INT: GOTHIC CHAMBER – NIGHT

We see GEORGE face down in the deserted chamber, now
arranged

...

That was it. That was the bottom of the last page. George turned the heavy pile of white paper over to check for folded pages. He rested the script on his forearm, gripping the crisp sheets firmly at the top from behind and flicking through them, desperately searching for a missing last page, looking for the ending. How does it end!!?

There was nothing there. He dropped the bedraggled paper onto the canvas chair with a plump. He noticed a leather riding whip on the floor next to the chair. A discarded prop perhaps, or the whip of a commanding auteur? He turned slowly to look at the set, this once feared room that was now mere decoration.

There was no ceiling. The edge of the thin walls revealed them to be board, supported from behind on a weak metal frame. Flimsy foam walls.

On the wall opposite the wooden chair, the two torches were still burning, flanking the two doors: one white and one black. The red velvet curtain was piled on the floor, exactly where the interrogator had left it.

"One is life, the other death..." recalled George.

There was nothing else to do, he had to choose a door. White would be too obvious for life, and black for death... but perhaps by being too obvious white really is life and black actually death. Or, it might be a triple bluff, where white is death and black is life because the inverse would be a trick on being too obvious.

The correct door was impossible to calculate.

He moved closer to the white door and touched the wood. It seemed solid enough. The wall here was cool, gritty, like actual stone. The rusted iron bands that supported the torches were nailed into the sandy wall. At least something here was real. He raised a fist to test a door with a knock, then paused. What if a knock was to choose, to request an opening like a spectral traveller calling: "Is there anybody there?"

He stepped back, between both doors, and brought his hands to his lips, palms together, as though in prayer. Which to choose? He tapped his forefingers together to mark the beat of his thoughts. Perhaps he could open one, just a crack. Just a tiny crack to peek beyond. A glimpse of blue light would be day, and blackness night. He will choose the white door.

George stepped forwards, and grabbed the cool iron ring that marked the handle. He rattled it, then turned it anticlockwise. It moved smoothly. It was well oiled, and an unseen latch on the other side of the door lifted. There was no lock; a gentle push, light and soft, would ease it open. Carefully, slowly, he pushed into the door, still clasping the ring tightly. Suddenly the door pulled violently at his arm, the door tearing itself open and pulling him in with it. Air began to rush past George, sucked into the opening, creating a powerful wind which boomed and hissed towards the black void, the gap barely wide enough for a man to fit though. George leaned back and flailed out his free arm, grabbing the stone wall on the hinge side of the door, gripping a lump of coarse rock. The torch by his side blew out in the wind, sending a flat line of smoke running, like a beam from the hot dead wood, through the wind storm, towards the gap, and into the icy pit of nothingness beyond the door.

George's hand remained clamped on the iron ring and his arm was being pulled, torn painfully by the force of the wrestling door. He bent his knees, and tugged at the door, using his arm like a rope to winch it closed. It was working. The door was slowly being pulled back, giving way. He heaved once more, pushing down hard with his bent arm, and then slammed the door closed with a mighty boom. The wind stopped. He twisted the handle with his sore arm to close the latch. The smoke from the extinguished torch swirled, puffing a blue carbon ring into space, and then relaxed, sending a smooth line upwards that rippled and riffled into waves of brief excitement, and then calm, vaporous, nothingness.

He cradled his aching forearm in the other, massaging soothing circles into the burning muscles with his thumb.

The black door it must be.

George stepped to the side and reached out to touch the cold metal handle. As soon as the tips of his fingers made a tiny contact with the door, it fell away, like a domino tumbling in space, knocked casually from a tabletop, turning and rolling like the arcs and wheels traced in the air by the tips of shivering ferns or the bobbing leaves of a desert plant, gently nodding like a ballerina taking a bow, or conducting a waltz. Away fell the door into blackness. End over end. Blinking in reflected white light until its tiny speck had receded away and away into infinite darkness.

George put his shoulder on the stone edge of the rectangular hole and leaned in to peer into the void beyond.

"Sorry, I can't do it! I can't push him," said a voice. "The script, the original synopsis of this play, says that I should kick George into the hole. A final message that escaping death is impossible and that any choices are illusory, but no. I can't do it. I refuse."

Behind, and to the side of George was the interrogator, now hatless and clutching a fluttering script. He looked different, more kindly. The darkness around his eyes was now more obviously make-up. He reached to George's back shoulder and gently touched it, bringing the hapless protagonist out of his daydream. George turned around. The guard was now a woman, middle-aged with tussled flames of long red hair. Her face had freckles and a kindly smile, and she was wearing a flowing white gown of translucent gossamer material.

"Come..." she said softly, and held out her hand.

George took it and began to feel a lightness in his shoulders. Ripples of tension flipped away in rings, like a million prickling mousetraps, triggered in pond-circles that emitted from the hollows in his back. Behind the wave was the most beautiful feeling of softness and smoothness. Relaxation and calmness. He inhaled deeply, and the air tasted as fresh as pure oxygen, clear blue, like the mountain breezes that fly and cycle over clean glaciers. A wonderful glow of peace spread from his neck, along his chest to his shoulders, and down his arms, now light and relaxed. The soft feeling dripped, like honey rain, slowly down the front of his body, to his navel, his legs and feet, which felt warm, liquid, insubstantial, as though his lower half was made from the matter of love. Up into the air he floated, like a balloon released by a child, slowly, gently and with lightness. Up, into a free sky that grew warmer with each breath, more beautiful with each movement skywards; from darkness to a rich blue, like the colour of warm ocean water. From rich blue to light blue, and into a fresh, summer sky, free from the mist of soft clouds, and up further, higher and higher, in warmth and peace, into infinite distance.

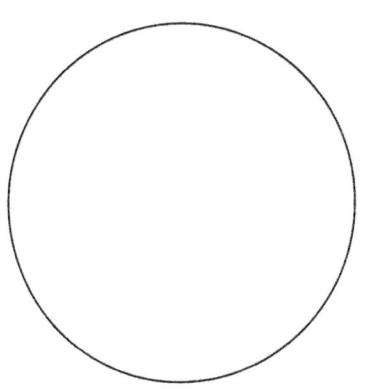